DIRTY WINGS

FELICIA FOX

Published by Felicia Fox - Hot Ink Press

Cover done by Rue Volley

Edited by Catherine Stovall

Formatted by Kristen Hope Mazzola

❀ Created with Vellum

FOREWORD

To my wonderful readers, you are the reason I have continued putting my worlds, heart, and bits of my soul into the written word. Thank you for going on this journey with Celine and I as she dares to go for what she wants. Consequences be damned.

Most dangerous
is that temptation that doth goad us on
to sin in loving virtue.

William Shakespeare

CHAPTER 1

"I am going to be strong this time. I will not succumb. I will detach myself and do my job, watch. You can do this Celine. This is not your first assignment, and he will not be your last." I repeat this mantra to myself *over* and *over* again.

I am an Angel. Part of the Heavenly Watcher ranks. We monitor souls teetering on the edge of going completely black and needing to be dragged off to hell by our Enforcers. I have been a Watcher for the last two-thousand heavenly years, and I love my calling. It gives me purpose and brings me joy.

Right now, I am trying to zone my sight in on him. Leviathan Drayce Deveraux, or Levi as he likes to be called. He is a half-breed demon who likes to test the limits of his freedom. Levi has been my charge for twenty human years which translates to two heavenly years, and it is...interesting to say the least.

I lie on my back and glance down at my arms before I cross them over my chest. I observe the difference of color between my pale ivory skin and the fluffy white cloud surrounding me. It helps to slowly trance myself onto the earthly plane. I focus on Levi. The crisp vision of his six-foot-two frame presents itself in my mind's eye.

Levi is in a candle-lit room. The walls are painted black, giving it a feel of unending stasis. He *plays* with his prey in this member's only establishment. The light from the candles' flame dances upon his hair, making it shine like obsidian. It hangs to his shoulders in waves and covers his face while he whispers in newest conquest's ear. He has a ball-gag in the woman's mouth, the leather straps pressing into her cheeks. Her plump, ruby-colored lips pull back, and her perfect teeth sink into the black ball as she sucks in a breath.

"You're *mine* to do with as *I* please." His voice is deep, gravely, and mesmerizing.

It makes me shiver in anticipation for what he will say next.

Levi glides his full sinful lips over the shell of her ear, biting and tugging at the lobe. "Nod yes."

She does, with great enthusiasm.

After a moment of looking upon her, I see her life play out in quick detail. Like watching a film in fast forward, details blur but emotions and actions remain clear. In just a blink of time, I know the woman's name is Bette Farnsworth. This young woman is thirty-two years old and an only child, parents deceased. She resides in a large city where she owns her own advertising company. Bette lives lavishly but gives her time and large amounts of her funds to charity. I also know that, even with all her money, she is still painfully lonely. Bette is a good person and would not need a Watcher's constant eye.

I will call in one of the Joy Bringers to help guide her after she and Levi are done. No need corrupting the Joy Bringers sight.

Bette's groaning around the ball-gag brings my full attention back to the scene. Levi is beginning his slow, sexual torment of her. Bending over Bette's curvaceous body, he teases her with his mouth, softly biting his way down her abdomen. The candle light gleams over Levi's golden skin and makes me salivate for a taste of him. I want to trace the lines of his lean muscular build with light sweeping grazes of my fingers.

Oh, sweet deity, not again!

I quickly shut down my connection to him and open my eyes. My pupils sting at the sudden brightness of my home. I stare out into the endless, misty white surroundings.

What am I doing?

I am lusting after my charge, that's what. This is my dirty secret. If the Council finds out, I will be let go from my calling, or worse. I will become one of the *Fallen.* To be Fallen is to have our grace stripped away and to be sent through the veil to live out a human existence. No hope of earning your wings back. Once they are severed, they can never be replaced.

I shiver at the thought of living a short, mortal life. An existence filled with pain and yearning for the serenity of our heavenly home is torture. Knowing not one of my people would remember who I am to them saddens me. I do not want to feel the loss of my grace forever. Even in death, the Fallen are kept separate from our brethren, almost invisible. The Council makes sure it is enforced as well.

Our Great Deity may be a being of forgiveness,

but the Council is not. They are the be-all and end-all in decisions concerning our angel ranks. Unforgiving in their verdicts, they will strip the wings and grace from an angel without blinking an eye. Some say they are created to have no empathy. Watching the way they pass judgment, I can see how that may be true.

I sigh deeply and close my eyes. The slight breeze blows the waves of my white-blonde, hip-length hair around my tall and slender body. I feel weightless, floating in my fluffy cloud. It tickles the exposed skin on my arms.

Breathe deep. Exhale. Now, do your job. Detach yourself.

I gasp when the vision of them enters my mind once more. Bette writhes from Levi's ministrations. His moves are calculated and controlled to bring the utmost pleasure with pain.

A familiar tingle dances in the pit of my stomach. I begin to lightly stroke up and down my arms with the tips of my wings. They curl around my body, responding to the excess of stimuli. I remind myself to detach, but I can't help wanting to feel. My feathers flutter excitedly all over my body and through the cool fluffiness surrounding me. My slim figure shivers in delight. My own nipples bead instantly as my temptation works Bette's body over with his strong, masculine hands.

She is pale and perspiration slick. Her body is in shackles, spread-eagled on a St. Andrews Cross. Each section of the dark wooden cross is adjustable to allow the body to stretch open wider. Her platinum blonde hair, the color similar mine, is tied back in a bun. Wisps of her locks stick to her face. Seeing the similarities between Bette and my own appearance makes it easy to replace her with myself in this vision. Instead of her sky-blue eyes shining with unshed tears, they are the deep emerald green of mine. The thought has my legs slightly scissoring together, and an ache begins to throb inside my sex.

Long, red welts crisscross over her full breasts and thighs from the leather braided flogger he has in his hand. Casually, he brings the instrument down against Bette's body, making her whimper one last time. He throws the flogger to the table against the wall. Her chest rises and falls at an alarming rate, but the yearning in her eyes indicates excitement.

Levi grips the chain connecting her breasts together, pulling the blushing pink nipples taut as he slams himself into her dripping wet sex. He runs his other hand over the now raised marks on Bette's tender red flesh. The pain and pleasure make her squirm against him. His golden skin glistens with a light sheen of sweat. The colorful dragon tattoo wrapping around his bicep and forearm seems to move with each graceful stroke of his arm.

Levi throws his head back, and my breath catches as his eyes are revealed. I grasp the iridescent fabric of the gown I wear in my fists to stop me from touching myself. The smooth silk is a poor substitution for the flesh I wish to have my hands on. I stop listening to Levi and Bette in their throes of passion. I fear it will be too much stimulation for me to handle, and I will succumb to finding my own release.

Levi's golden, lion-colored eyes turn fierce. His thrusts pound harder into her willing core. It makes my feathers tingle all the way to their pristine white tips as his grip tightens on the chain.

I, as an angel, should abhor sadistic acts that bring this twisted sort of pleasure to the abused.

Heaven help me!

Tears flow from Bette's eyes, but I sit here and covet the emotions and sensations she endures.

Bette finally surrenders, with his permission, to the orgasm he has been denying her over and over again. Her muscles convulse as her body processes the intensity of her long-awaited climax. It is mind bending to see the woman content and not furious over Levi's treatment of her body. The weight of the world seems to lift off Bette's shoulders as she lays limply against the cross. Her head lolls to the side, and his seed drips down her thighs. She is at peace.

I take a deep breath of the cool air to calm my racing heart. Maybe it is time to admit I need a new assignment. Levi is making me question my calling. He makes me hunger for sensations I have never in my lifetime wanted or even thought of. When he came into his powers, I was assigned to be Levi's Watcher. For twenty human years, I have patiently waited for the day Leviathan's foot slips over the line he recklessly toes.

He will slip. They always do. Then Levi will lose all the privilege his half-breed status gives him. He will be sent into the fiery pits to live the rest of his existence with his father, Malacoda, and I will send him there. The thought of being the one to decide his fate is an extremely somber one. It is confusing to have these twisted emotions interfering with my calling.

Malacoda is a high-ranking demon, for Pete's sake. He is worshiped as the Prince of Pain and Agony because he takes sustenance from the suffering he inflicts and the fiery depths of Hell is his playground.

Leviathan inherited that nasty little trait. He learned to satiate his hunger with his sexually deviant pleasures. Still free to roam Earth, he has no powers. He is made weak by his hunger for pain. His appetite seems to be growing steadily as he ages. It worries me, but I see the light in him. His soul still shines brightly, and it gives me hope—though the odds are stacked against him.

Bette has no inkling that she is *feeding* a half-breed demon, but I know he is taking nourishment from her. A tiny speck of my being is envious of Bette. Envy, is one of the big no-no's for according to heavenly commandments. Then again, so is lust. I should just be a good angel, bind myself to one of my own kind, and live a peaceful Watcher's life.

I throw my head back into my cloud to shake the thoughts from my mind.

I refocus on Levi as he brings a bowl and cloth over from his side table. He stands in front of Bette and softly bathes her while she is still held up on the cross. Levi does this to temper the guilt he feels from feeding. He is very vigilant in his care of the submissive woman and does this after every encounter.

In this moment, concern and gratefulness comes

off him in invisible waves. They wrap around her body and soul. The half-breed, has a peace about him after this release of sexual tension. There is clarity in his eyes and grace in his movements now that the veil of hunger has rose.

Levi gently dries the woman and rubs lotion onto areas of her body he whipped. He takes her off the cross and lays her on the white linens covering the single bed. He stands and slowly looks around.

He must feel my presence. Oh no!

I open my eyes again and take in my surroundings. I need to visit Marcus. He is my mentor and friend. I will see if it is possible or wise to hand off Levi to another Watcher. He will most likely be in his cloud. I think of the male, and in the blink of an eye, I am standing no more than two-feet from him. He smiles as he opens his quicksilver eyes. Marcus is a beautiful male, but all angels are. He closes the distance between us, his arms are raised to embrace me. Stepping into the warmth of Marcus, comfort washes through me.

"Hello, sweetling. I have missed you." His voice is like silk, so smooth.

I melt against his hard-muscular physique just a little.

"I have been keeping a close watch on my charge. His hunger is…" I stop myself. I do not want him to worry. He will send for The Enforcers, and in a heartbeat, they will smite Levi. "His hunger is increasing and…" I just cannot finish the thought aloud. A lie will be too obvious, and it tastes horrible on my tongue.

"I see. What is making you uncomfortable?" A tick starts at the corner of his full lips. One that only appears when he is trying his hardest not to smile.

While I withhold my response, his body shakes. The short platinum hair on his head vibrates as he tries to hold back his mirth. Heat floods my face as I blush red.

He knows why and is teasing me. Well, two can play that game. I won't let him think I am a meek female.

"It is Leviathan's use of sex and pain at the same time." I didn't have to wait long for his reaction.

He laughs so hard, he doubles over, wings sticking out. I smile, even if I am a little embarrassed. His joy is infections. Marcus's cloud brightens with his mood to highlight his angelic nature to an extreme, and my wings flitter in response.

"I have peeked in on him, too and wondered when you would come running to me. I knew you would want me to transfer you." he says through gasps of breath as his laughter continues.

"You have been keeping tabs on me? You didn't have faith I could do this on my own?" Marcus's doubt in my abilities hurts. He makes me feel like a newling, though I have been doing this job for years. "I am a Watcher, the same as you, and have seen many things. Why, of all my charges, is this one a concern to you?" My voice shakes with suppressed emotions.

"My sweetling," he says sympathetically, making me feel all the worse for it, "I was ordered to keep an eye on you and your charge. He is the son of a greater demon, and you cannot tell me he is like any of your other charges."

I open my mouth to tell him he is wrong, but he raises his hand to stop me from interrupting,

"Yes, you have had to send The Enforcers after souls that have gone dark but nothing ever like this."

I take a deep breath, knowing he is right. This was why I came to him today. I want a transfer but not because of embarrassment. I fear I will want more than just the visions of Levi. I make a decision then and there that I *will* do this job, and I *will* endure the hungers that come along with it. In fact, I am going to go one step further.

"I am going to cross the veil onto the earthly plane," I say quickly and close my eyes to mist back to my cloud.

"You most certainly are not going," Marcus says, grabbing my arm and preventing me from leaving.

I try to tug away, but his grip is like steel, shackling me in place.

"I am going!" I sound like a petulant child. I know he is probably right, but I need to do this now. I need to prove I am more than capable of handling a half-breed demon. Even if this particular one tempts me on a level I have never before experienced.

"Is there something you are not telling me, Celine?" His grip loosens slightly, and an edge of worry hangs in his voice.

I think I see maybe even a secret or two slither through his churning silver eyes.

"No, I came here to talk to you about Leviathan's increase in hunger, and to tell you I will be going to monitor him." The half lie tastes bitter, and I want to spit the vile acid out of my mouth like liquid.

"Will you make yourself fully corporal to watch him?"

Marcus's question is a serious one, and has every right as my friend and mentor to ask.

"No! Of course not! I will just mist around him.

He may feel or suspect my presence, but that should be the extent." I would never expose myself on purpose. My wings would be too vulnerable in human state. It is forbidden as well. Unless you are helping souls cross over into heaven's undying fields.

I smile, wanting to let go of the hurt I feel over Marcus keeping tabs on me.

"Please, come home the moment you feel the slightest doubt about your safety." He pulls me in close, tightening his arms around me once again.

The warmth of his body and soul wrap around me in this extended embrace. Marcus looks deep into my eyes, and for the first time, I feel a slight tension in his hold.

Does he desire me, or is it just residual feelings from having watched Levi?

I gently pull away from Marcus's hold. His quick-silver eyes swirl enticingly, beckoning me to fall into him and swim in their depths.

"I will come if my life is in danger. I promise," I say patiently, stepping away before I succumb to this confusing urge.

"Good bye, my sweetling." A small, sad smile plays upon his lips.

I should feel some empathy for him, but the excitement of going through the veil over-shadows it. I close my eyes to send myself back to my own space when I feel the tethering of Marcus's hand in my own. I jump, startled by the unexpected touch. I look up into his face and am taken back by the intensity of his gaze.

"Marcus, is something amiss?" I cock my head to the side in confusion.

"I do not want you to think I have no faith in your abilities. I care for you greatly," he says in a voice as coaxing as it is comforting. Like a cooing one would do toward a skittish animal.

The tone makes me want to forgive him anything.

"May I accompany you for the first day, sweetling? Just to reassure myself of your safety."

Marcus's earnest request makes me feel terrible for having doubted his faith in me. He truly cares for me, as I do for him. I will not deny my greatest friend and mentor such a reasonable request. Given the fact he asks instead of watching because he can and he wants to, makes me adore him that much more.

"You are absolutely welcome to come with me." I smile and see the tension he is holding in his shoulders dissipate. "I will send for you before I leave." I wrap my arms around him in a quick hug, and this time, there is no hindrance when I go to mist away.

Exuberance and trepidation battle inside me for dominance, but it looks like curiosity is stepping in to win. For the first time in my two-thousand heavenly years of life, I will be amongst the human populace. I will be a shade closer to Levi. Can I remain strong enough to not reach out and touch him? Will I stop myself from going corporal so I may feel life as it flows on Earth? Oh, Deity, give me power to resist my temptation.

Back on my home, I make an impulsive decision to have one more look at Levi before I go. Just one more peek from the safety of my cloud. I zone in on him immediately. My focus is razor sharp in my excitement.

Levi enters his bathroom. He steps shakily into the shower, turning the nozzle and letting the stream hit him. He winces, leaning his head into the steady pounding of the overhead nozzle. Water sluices off his sculpted body to whirl hypnotically around the drain. He grabs the bar of soap off the little ledge and scrubs his body.

Levi's well-defined muscles trembles as he lathers the little amber bar of soap into his hands. The steam quickly thickens in the room, slightly obscuring my view of Levi. I center my attention too hard, almost passing through the veil to see him more clearly. What I witness is so achingly sad. I wish I would have given him this moment to himself.

Levi's hands move at a blurring speed, scrubbing his skin red in the scalding heat. Heaving breaths make his chest pump up and down franticly.

"Count, Levi. One, you can't help but feed." He does one quick path over his body, starting with his face and working his way down to his toes, "Two, you are not dirty." Levi lathers his hands again and repeats the same circuit—much slower this time, "Three, it'll all be over one day." This time, he stands, just letting the water wash it all away. "Four, you're not your father." Levi's breathing calms as he repeats this to himself three times over.

I want to reach out and wrap him in my arms and wings. I want to tell him he is strong, and he is not alone. Levi leans his forehead against the tile, shoulders hunched over, and shudders.

Even though this moment is one of anguish, it instills more strength in my hope for Leviathan, son of Malacoda.

CHAPTER 3

I take a deep breath of the misty air and try to settle the emphatic feelings I have for Levi's situation. I know from all of my time watching, he is torn between what he wants to be and what he could become. The half-breed looks exhausted by it all. I summon my cloud to make a forest for myself. I walk among the trees, collecting my thoughts before I send a call out to Marcus for us to depart.

One more reason not to fall. My beautiful home. My cloud that lets me have any scene I wish to see. I can stare at the hypnotic waves one minute and the tallest mountains the next. Although I cannot feel the breeze playing among the leaves and the sun beaming against the oceans waves, I still have the most resplendent views. Truly, our Great Deity is an artist of unparalleled talent.

Being here, in the heavenly realm, I've no need for sustenance. Food and drink are a source of curiosity for me, but they are absolutely unnecessary for an Angel. Though I may wish to feel why such abundance brings joy to the person consuming them, I think masticating would be a bit icky.

All of these jumbled thoughts pass through me, and suddenly, the picture of Levi with the woman Bette enters my mind. My body heats. The way he caresses her while she is strung up for hers and his pleasure. Surprisingly, this flash of heat is for an entirely different reason than has ever hit me before. It makes my stomach clench and my hands curl into my garment, fisting the delicate material. I am afraid to admit this is a stirring of jealousy. An emotion unfamiliar to me.

Once, in the beginning of my bourgeoning attraction to him, I was so close to alleviating the pressure between my thighs while I watched him slowly enter one of his companions. I shake the memory away and instead picture his hand gently cradling the back of my head as his lips slowly descend toward mine.

I shake the thought away and find my hands are roaming my body. Immediately, I panic. *No wonder Marcus worries for me.*

Maybe I really am not to be trusted. Will I sacrifice all for a taste of these sensations? I do not think I can go through with the actions, but only our Great Deity knows for sure. I will regard these emotions as nerves. After all, I am about to be on the Earthly plane—just as soon as I send my call out to Marcus.

Now is the time.

"I am ready," my mind whispers across the distance of our two dwellings.

Instead of responding in kind, he appears by my side. I smile from the warmth of this beautiful being next to me. His holy light bathes me in calm and serenity and is another reminder of the total love, understanding, and comradery of my brethren.

"Are you truly ready, my sweetling?"

"I am, Marcus. I have existed for two-thousand heavenly years. It is absurd I have not made this journey even once before this case."

He smirks and takes my hand, "Well then, let us go. Shall we?"

I close my eyes and tie myself to his psyche, so I will mist into the same place as he. The sensation of crossing planes is like an electric current through my body. I feel as if my nerve endings are coming out of a deep sleep. A miraculous as well as concerning sensation. When traversing heaven, it's more of a thought and you appear. A nothingness, I guess.

Already, the movement from one place to the other has brought to mind a question I will have to think on further, when away from Marcus. I am so focused on the feeling, I almost mist completely into the reality of the Earthly plane.

The sun. My Deity! It is so tantalizing in its warmth, and the slight wind is instantly refreshing. It is a symphony as the elements battle for attention. Birdsong is so clear, it vibrates the currents of air. The music makes me tingle as I absorb its sound waves.

I remember I am under the veil of Marcus's mist and snap back into the situation at hand. I look over at him, and he has his infuriating little smirk on his handsome face.

So much for being able to pass onto this plane for the first time without aid.

Why does he always have to be right?

"Can you please be a bit more supportive, Marcus?" I ask in a self-depreciative mumble.

"If you will pay more attention to your surroundings, I will be happy to."

"I am well aware of how distracted I am," I say while looking around. My vision is filled and my senses bombarded by all the sensory waves flowing around my being.

I take a deep breath and work hard to tune out all that's happening around me. When I open my eyes, I notice we are in the little outside market Levi comes to on occasion.

And there *he* is, the sun shining down on him. The glowing rays highlight his inner light as well, making my heartbeat trip over itself and my wings flutter. I even unintentionally squeeze Marcus's hand, and his gaze levels on me as I stare—transfixed on Levi.

His gait is smooth and almost predatory. He effortlessly glides through the throng of people. His skin is sun kissed, and his body accented by the clothes that hug him in an absolutely masculine and unarguably inviting manner. There is a softness to the worn looking material. I want to caress the fabric as much as I want to touch the man it encases. His golden eyes are hidden by dark-lensed sunglasses, and I ache for a glimpse of them.

"Celine, are you sure you want to leave the safety of your home to follow him around?"

I try to tear my gaze away, but his question goes unanswered as I watch a young woman approach Levi. Sable hair streams behind her in the slight breeze. Her face is made up of graceful lines and the lightest of facial adornments. Lip gloss, I believe. She is short in stature with lovely, dewy skin—darkened by the sun. She is without the curves maturity and time brings to most women.

I focus on the young woman and her life flashes quite quickly. Her eighteen years of existence are sweet and comfortable. Such innocence and well-intentioned behavior. She is genuinely kind and giving, with parents who are supportive and loving. The peace and love instilled in her is tangible on this plane. I want to dive into her light and let it soak into me. She will become a great healer, and her touch will comfort many.

Her name whispers through my mind. *Marisol....* And, at the moment, she is looking for *adventure* and thinks to find it this summer before she goes off to college. She is determined to move away from this sleepy little town of Tess, Oregon and from her goody-two-shoes image. To achieve this new start,

Marisol decides she needs some sexy older man to give her "V" card to.

It takes me a moment to realize what she means by that thought, and when I do I heat, knowing exactly why she approaches Levi.

I no longer care that she is a genuinely kind soul as my blood begins to simmer. Now, I see her as young, nubile, and so very touchable to him. Absolutely corruptible when she has such a bright future ahead of her. Maybe, I should use this opportunity to influence her away. Even though it is against heavenly law for a Watcher to affect the decisions of the human race. I immediately change my mind. No need to have a council verdict to answer to.

Freewill an endowment to the human populace—a gift to do with as they please, and a way to better learn of the True Deity's lessons for life. Experience being the teacher for his grand plan for all on the other side of the veil. Even I, an angel, do not know what the end is. But I know my place, and I'm content in following.

At this very moment, I am willing to risk it. Just throw it all away to save the young woman. Truly this is about *her* and not the fact Levi may touch another woman when I am this close. At least I will keep telling myself this.

Despite these stirring feelings and thoughts, the more practical side of me knows Levi will be a great first lover for her. He will be kind once he has taken her maidens head and will gently push her in another direction if she wants more than a few trysts. Practicality is not enough to sooth the ache in the center of my being when I think of the two of them together.

I try to listen to their conversation but turn as Marcus's voice intrudes once again. I've no idea what he asks so I reply with a, "Hmm...?"

As I gaze up at his stern face, he shakes his head in frustration.

"I should take you home right now. You have no idea what you are getting yourself into, do you?"

No, not at all, I think to myself but answer him differently. "Yes. Yes, I do," I respond on a deep exhale. "You've no need to stay with me. I am quite capable. I'm even known to do my job well." My voice holds zero inflection as I let the dry sarcasm answer his impatient look.

Marcus's chiseled jaw clenches even harder than usual as he peers down at me. A cloud overhead passes, uncovering the sun's nourishing rays. The beams of light suddenly catch Marcus's brilliance.

I am suddenly speechless. His heavenly light is

magnificent, and I wonder if he sees the same in me as his features soften.

He reaches a hand out and places it on my shoulder. The touch firm but not aggressive. His eyes close as he shakes off some deep emotion trying to take him over.

"I will leave you to your work, Celine. But, please, take care."

I wrap my hand around his wrist to solidify my answer. "Of course, I will, my dear Marcus."

He nods and is gone in the next beat of my heart. I stand still for a while, feeling the sensation of the sun soak into my epidermis in this half-corporal state but making sure not to slip completely through. The feel of it against my porcelain skin is absolutely sublime. The warmth seeps its way into my body makes me languid and buoyant at the same time. I relish the newness and the emotions it brings forth.

I know I have taken on much more than I bargained for as I experience these new sensations. *I must focus,* I say to myself. There is a devilishly handsome man to follow around. Heavy emphasis on the devilish part. Hopefully, he has shunned the young girl by the time I look upon him again.

My eyes automatically find him, as I am so

attuned to his soul. I walk the short distance to where he sits on a bench. Alone, thank all that is holy. Although. I am curious as to what he may have said to Marisol. I want to look into his mind and see the conversation they engaged in, but it is impossible. Being part demon or angel in any fashion makes a being immune to mind reading and life mapping. Levi's thoughts are a mystery to me, and I am more than happy to give him that privacy.

Did he accept the invitation from her or did he reject her? The question bounces around my mind. I feel a slight pang over her probable rejection. I know if I am ever in the same situation, I will find myself mortified. The idea of being turned away after finding the strength to voice my want has my stomach in a knot.

Levi stares at the screen on his sleek phone with a look of irritation on his face. I close in and see the subtle stiffening of his body. Shoulders tense, he taps his phone with a skilled and furious pace. I walk around him and try to look over his shoulder, but before I can do so, he whips the device down and into the back pocket of his pants.

Oh, Deity, I am close enough I can smell him—like crisp clean air and the slightest hint of spice. It is intoxicating, and I inhale deeply. I watch his body twitch, and I immediately back up, worried my presence here is bothersome. I walk around the bench once again and stand in front of him, willing him to look upon me. I know the trouble such an action will cause, but I cannot help myself. He tilts his head back. and I can almost feel his gaze—even though I know it cannot be true. With the sunglasses shielding his eyes, I will never know.

I watch Levi take in a breath, and it seems to be caught in his chest. I wonder what the reason is. I turn around to see if he is gazing upon Marisol. If she is the reason for such a reaction…. I stop myself, though the curiosity presses upon me even more so than before. This is not what I am here for.

You are stronger than this. You will work through all of these new sensations, and you will watch Levi, not pine after him, I remind myself harshly.

After all, Levi is a half demon. I, as a heavenly Watcher, will be responsible for bringing the Enforcers down on him. What love can he have for someone who is to sentence him to an eternity in hell beside his father. There is no future for the two of us, and the thought is sobering. I would lose Heaven and the only family I have ever known if I stray from the path I have been gifted. To turn my back on what the Creator has blessed me with would be blasphemy, and I do not want to be party to that.

I repeat my mantra to myself. *I am going to be strong this time. I will not succumb. I will detach myself, and do my job. I will watch. You can do this, Celine. This is not your first assignment, and he will not be your last."*

CHAPTER 4

"Can I get a coffee, black?" Levi asks while handing his money to the cashier.

The orchestra of sound echoing through this little coffee shop is almost deafening. I inhale deeply. The smell of roasted beans suffusing this establishment is absolutely sublime. Levi is on edge today and is short with the young man behind the counter.

The lanky-limbed cashier has a bored look on his face while pushing the buttons on the monitor. The white embroidered tag on his apron says his name is Andrew. I close my eyes and his life flashes in my mind.

The red-haired young man is a twenty-three-year-old college drop-out. Andrew lives with his grandmother in her tiny, two-bedroom home just a mile away. He has an addiction to prescription pills and uses his grandmother for access to them.

I have hope for Andrew. He still has a long life in which to find redemption. *Poor soul will suffer grievously for his treatment of his Grandmother, but it will be of his own doing.*

Levi nods at Andrew while taking the coffee before weaving in and out of the line of people still waiting for their order and making his way out of the little shop.

It is bright out as we exit the coffee shop. The tiny bell above the door rings, making me feel a little giddy. Oh, the small joys of being on this side of the heavens. The sun's gleaming rays make Levi squint his eyes. He puts on his dark sunglasses again. I am starting to not like them. They hide so much of the expression on his face. Alas, he has taken to wearing them often these days.

Levi's shoulder-length hair is tied back today, and it shines like ebony glass. My eyes trace the colorful dragon tattoo clearly visible under his body-hugging black tank top. The dragon wraps around his bicep, the tail curling around and down his forearm in a kaleidoscope of different hues.

The people's eyes gravitate to Levi. They watch

him saunter down the street with his smooth and confident steps. Women and men stare, finding his features arresting to their senses. He ignores their attention. I know it is because he would rather go unnoticed.

He sips his coffee, cursing that it's still too hot to drink and dribbling a bit of it onto his jeans. I giggle like a small child. He stiffens and walks just a tiny bit faster, and I am quite sure it's from feeling my presence.

I have now been following Levi around for a couple of weeks. Today is the first time I have seen him in such a foul mood. He is not only cranky but also extremely busy as he prepares for his monthly "meeting". It is the first of July, and usually, the beginning of the month is the hardest on Levi because he often opens a small window-like portal into hell and speaks to his father.

I know he usually needs to feed soon after these encounters, and I have come to believe that Malacoda forces the hunger on Levi in some way. It could just be the stress and being so close to hell that brings it on as well. Whatever the reason for the increase, Malacoda uses it to strengthen his belief that, if Levi learns to indulge in his hungers, he will come home sooner.

Levi won't deny Malacoda these visits. After all, the demon is Leviathan's father. Malacoda, a prince of hell, has few offspring and wants his progeny ruling his realms of hell at his side. I am sure he would approve of any attempt at bringing his son to him.

Levi runs a bar called Hell's Gates, appropriately named for what Levi does in his office during this time of month. The bar is in a rougher and decaying part of this small town. Graffiti fills the walls and broken glass-bottles and trash sporadically line the streets. A couple of men lie passed out in the alley with only cardboard and layers of dirt-caked clothes to keep them safe from the elements. It makes my heart clench for their circumstances, knowing they are using the light of day as a security measure just to sleep with some form of peace.

Misting around the earthly plane is thrilling, even with all the sadness surrounding the places Levi inhabits. I go fully corporal for small moments of time so I can feel and touch everything. I know I shouldn't, but I cannot help myself. I wiggle my bare toes into the coarse carpet and relish its roughness. The feel of running water over my fingertips is exhilarating, and I shiver as I imagine what that sensation would be like all over my body. The firm bounce of a bed makes me want to jump with glee until my legs give out. I cannot do so for fear Levi would walk in and catch me. I make a promise to myself that, one day, I will.

I wonder if he can feel my presence more than he seems to let on. Occasionally, I will see his shoulders stiffen as I enter the same room. The veins in Levi's neck and arms stand out with strain when I come near him. The hardest part of being in such proximity to Levi is the desire to reach out and touch him.

Does it feel the same as when I reach out for one of my brethren? Would it be doubly as sensational as everything else is here?

I watch him as he engages in physical fitness routines that make my mouth water. When his obsidian hair falls haphazardly across his face, obstructing the view of his golden eyes, I have to restrain myself from pushing the strands back.

"Jake, what the fuck are you doing?" he yells at the man behind the bar as he walks in, stomping in his big, black motorcycle boots. Levi grins as he scares Jake into having to catch the glass he was trying to stack on the shelf.

"I'm doing laundry. What the hell else would I be doing?" Jake responds in his usual snarky tone.

He is normally like this around Levi, which the half-breed finds amusing and eggs it on. I know Jake suspects his boss is something more. He never voices it, but the doubt of Levi's humanity keeps him just a little cautious it seems. I see it in the slight widening of space he gives him at times.

Jake has to be sensitive to other-worldly beings. I catch him looking directly towards me. Sometimes, he tilts his head as if trying to figure out if I am there or just a figment of his imagination. His life does not flash for me. Though his soul burns brightly, his past is absent. I guess you can say we both look at one another with curiosity, even though he does not truly see me.

Jake is an alluring man, as evidenced by the plethora of women who surround him when his shift starts. I embarrassingly catch myself staring at his light sea-green eyes made brighter by his deeply tanned skin. Though his face and body hold masculine beauty in spades, there is a darkness or deep sadness I cannot put my finger on. He makes my soul ache as if I should know why and cannot remember. It nags at me almost as much as the mystery of Levi's thoughts. I strongly contemplate going back to the heavenly plane to look through the archives for Jake and his secret past.

Levi comes to stand next to him, and Jake no longer holds my gaze. I compare them side-by-side. Both are the same height, with bodies of sinewy grace ready to pounce at a moment's notice. Their choice of clothing is similar, except Jake wears a white-t-shirt. There is feral intensity in Levi's being that acts like a magnet to everything feminine in me, so I force my eyes to linger on Jake instead. I constantly need to remind myself that Levi is a one-way ticket to losing my wings.

"Look, I need to take care of some...things tonight. I need you to stay here and watch the bar. I'll be out of the office in time to count down the till at the end of the night." Levi sighs heavily.

I wish he would deny Malacoda.

"I got this, Levi. It's the first week of the month, and you usually have shit to do. By the way, there is a package on your desk. It came in today," Jake says, turning quickly back to his task of stacking.

"Can I ask you something?" Levi asks with a look of curiosity on his face.

Jake turns around, looking a little nervous. His eyebrows draw together, giving him that adorable wrinkle between his eyes. "Um...yeah, shoot."

"I see all these women throwing themselves at

you, but you always leave them alone. I know you aren't married."

Sighing deeply, Jake responds, "You're going to call me a pussy."

"What makes you think I don't call you that now?" Levi says, chuckling.

I swear I swoon just a little at the sound.

"Well, fuck!" He is silent for a moment, looking for the words to express himself. "I'm just tired of running through them. There is only one girl that truly matters to me, and she already consumes my life. But you know that, and she is already half way in love with you."

Jake growls at Levi a little, but he takes it in stride with a cocky little grin.

Jake rubs his buzzed cut hair and looks in my direction. "Besides, it doesn't do shit for me anymore. I want something real, not just some one-night receptacle." He shakes his head, appearing lost in some painful thought.

Levi sees it, and sympathetically changes the subject to one that makes my heart pound —and not in a good way.

"That's all good for me. I can't compete with your pretty face, so you can just send them my way."

Levi walks toward his office, and I follow at a

safe distance, having to mist through the door as it closes. The room is small, neatly organized, and sparsely decorated. Unlike the darkly painted cavernous feel of the bar, this room is stark white with only a large gilded mirror to decorate the left side, giving it the illusion of space.

He walks over to his large glass and gun-metal gray steel desk and picks up the small, brown paper-wrapped package Jake left there. Levi smiles while reading the address label. The first one to grace his face all day. My curiosity gets the better of me, and I come close to take a peek at the package. He shivers at my presence but doesn't let on that he knows I'm here. I continue to read the label on the box. Instead of opening it, he sets it aside. The address is from a Sophie M. Jayne. I try to search my thoughts for who she is, but the name rings no bell. He looks to the left, and I know it is time for him to speak to his father.

He pricks his finger, and as the blood begins to bead, he presses it to the mirror. He makes a symbol in the center that soaks into the looking glass. The surface begins to shimmer, and the picture of his father starts to come into focus. I must now leave and quickly.

CHAPTER 5

I mist out of the room immediately. If Levi's father gets his hands on me, he can drag me to hell with him. A slight tremble starts from the top of my head and travels down to the tips of my toes. Malacoda was once an angel, a Joy Bringer. He fell with Lucifer during the uprising because he was tired of constantly trying to bring joy into humans' lives and them disregarding it. They were never happy long enough, and so he relishes bringing agony now. He would greatly enjoy ripping the wings from me and doing unspeakable atrocities to my mind and body.

I slip back into the bar and see Jake is stocking the bottles and ticking things off on a clip board. I sit at a table in the corner and long for my cloud. The wooden chair beneath me is hard and ungiving, but it will have to do. I focus and try to trance myself into watching Levi's interaction with his father.

"Have you done as I asked?"

Malacoda's voice is smooth, comforting, and reminds me of Marcus. I feel a pang of home sickness once again. There is something more about Malacoda, something alluring. I cannot pin-point it, but it is the same effect Levi has. It is as if I have to be near him. It must be some kind of demon pheromone. It makes no sense to me when they would have no reason to work their wiles if they cannot see me.

"Yes, Father," he says, handing the package he received over to Malacoda.

I cannot believe I am getting to look at Malacoda for the first time. In all this time, watching Levi, I never once laid mine eyes upon him. Not that I see every single interaction Levi has, but the ones with his father are almost non-existent for me. Almost as if they are timed perfectly.

I have difficulty breathing as I look upon him. His face is finely boned, almost feminine, except for the strong jawline. His eyes are blood red, swimming with shadows that swirl in constant motion. From the waist up, he wears a finely tailored suit with a crisp, white shirt underneath that is buttoned to mid chest, exposing his golden skin. I look away quickly, remembering high demons were once angels too. Their angelic looks are just another tool in their arsenal.

"Good, Son. Are you ready to come home?" Malacoda's voice is satin smooth, coaxing, and not matching his facial expression. He runs a hand through his short, haphazardly spiked, inky black hair. His face now boasting a look of boredom.

I assume it is because he already knows Levi's answer.

"No, I still have years of life to live here. I want the sun, the moon, the air, and wind. Shit, I'll take the fucking grimy-ass alley behind this building." Levi raises his voice at his father which is something I have never imagined him being able to do.

Malacoda becomes more aggressive. Energy violently crackles around him. "Your place is at my side, Leviathan. You belong to me. Remember who you are speaking to. The foul language is truly unnecessary."

"I will stay here for as long as my life permits me to, and I will speak in any way I want to. Free will and all that," he says.

Inside I cheer him on. *Good, Levi! Be your own*

man! I am on the edge of my seat, ready to give a standing ovation as I watch him stand up to his father.

"You have the face of your stubborn mother." Malacoda says with a wistful tone. His crimson eyes cloud over with some distant and cherished memory, judging by the slight smirk on his face. "She would have been treated as a queen here," Malacoda says low and more to himself.

"Yes, I am sure she would have loved to have been amongst all the gore and screams. Sounds like a real party." Levi shakes his head. "Did you know nothing of my mother?"

"She would have lived forever. Instead, she chose to die a horrible death, from cancer of all things. Her precious God wasn't there to spare her that pain, was he?"

"She had her faith, and it was enough," Levi says, almost equally disgusted by his mother's choice.

I know, even ten years after her death, a piece of him is still angry with her for giving life to him when he had a higher chance of suffering in hell for all eternity.

"I guess it was. I will let you get back to your putrid little world," Malacoda says with a negligent wave of his hand and disappears from the mirror.

"Good bye, Father," Levi says to the empty mirror as the connection is severed. He slowly walks back to his desk and leans against it.

While he collects himself, I give him space.

I snap back to myself and breathe deeply of the stale beer smell and disinfectant spray. Old smoke clings to the fabric of the booths. When I open my eyes, I see Jake looking directly at me before he winks.

He sees me.

Oh no! I'm not corporal. How in the heavens is he seeing me? Impossible! This must be a trick of the imagination.

JAKE SMILES and is about to speak when Levi comes in. He looks away quickly and goes back to cleaning. Levi goes behind the bar, and broods as he starts counting the till.

"Jake, restock and you're good to go," Levi says over his shoulder while flipping through a stack of twenty-dollar bills.

"Are you sure?" Jake responds, throwing the cloth in his hand over his shoulder. Shock and wariness play slightly across his face.

"Yeah, I can get the last tables. Get to it before I

change my mind," Levi snaps, making Jake finally move.

"Okay, okay…" he says, resigned.

But I see the slight smirk on his beautiful face. Like a jaded little twist of his lips.

When Jake goes to the back to grab the stock, I follow him. He stops and stands in front of the wooden crates. His hand reaches to pull out a bottle of amber liquid. I shore up my courage to approach him.

"Can you see me, Jake?" I ask, still doubtful of what I saw. I, a Watcher, being not sure of what I see is almost laughable.

"Yes, I can," he says quietly, looking around as if he is afraid of someone seeing him talk to me. Although, to the average outsider, he will look crazy for having a conversation with the air in front of him. Since Levi does not know of my existence, it is an almost laughable notion.

"How long have you been able to see me?" I ask urgently, wondering just how vulnerable I have made myself by coming to the earthly plane.

"Since your misty form glided in behind Levi."

That darn awful smirk Marcus usually gives me when he knows something I do not settles on Jake's lips. Makes me want to kick him in the shin.

Where is that violent thought coming from?

"Do you know what I am?" I admit my tone is a bit testy, but it is from nervousness. What if The Council discovers I am going about all willy-nilly and unknowingly showing myself around?

"The wings give it away, princess," he says sarcastically while looking over my shoulder, making my feathers ruffle.

"Oh…I suppose they do," I say, twisting the fabric of my gown which is something I do when I am nervous. Such a bad and telling habit I must learn to break. I doubt it will happen, being that I am already two-thousand heavenly years old.

"Why have you not said anything?" My curiosity drives me to ask.

"I assume you're here to keep Levi and his hungers in check. You're a Watcher. You are definitely not an Enforcer."

He is right. Enforcers are eight feet tall, and I, at five-foot-eleven, am dwarfed by them. But how in the two worlds does he know about this?

"How—?" I begin to ask when he cuts me off.

"I am Fallen, princess," he says condescendingly.

That explains why I cannot see his life. He is erased from our kind. He is just a lost soul amongst the many. I wonder if I knew him and am suddenly filled with grief on his behalf.

"Why did you fall?" I whisper, sympathy I constricting my vocal chords.

"That is a tale for another day," he says, pulling two more bottles out of the crate and setting them on the table beside him. "Why do you follow Leviathan?"

"He is assigned to me," I say proudly, puffing out my chest a little. *Darn it!* Now I am displaying pride. I am so getting my wings taken.

"I haven't seen his soul on the brink of turning black. Are they just looking for an excuse to smite him?" He practically spits out his words, insulting me and in turn, making me raise my voice.

"No! Not at all!" I am appalled Jake would think so badly of his former people. He should know better.

"Then why are you out of your cloud?"

He looks at me, and I feel naked. I am so afraid he will see the true reason for being here is to test myself against my greatest temptation.

"I...I..."

His face lights up with a mischievous grin as he steps closer to me. So close I can smell the sweet mint of the gum he was chewing earlier. His sea-green eyes are arresting, and I become entranced in their depths. There swimming in their depths is pain and an aching vulnerability that I now understand is loss.

Will my eyes look like this if my lusts are found out and my wings and grace are ripped from me?

"I think a sweet little angel saw something that caught her attention." Jake's voice deepens and coaxes me to lean in just a little closer.

My hands once again wrap in my gown as he continues.

"Maybe it was something hot and sweaty. Are you in…need?" He reaches a hand up toward my face, trying to prove a point. Just a sliver of air separates his skin from touching mine.

The heat from his hard, sinewy body radiates in waves against my own. The thought of bodily contact is an aching pulse of need inside of me. *How much more magnified will the sensations be if he closes the distance between us?* If I lean toward him just a fraction more, I can answer that question for myself.

"I wonder if I can touch you. I can see you." His smile widens. "Let's give it a try."

I close my eyes, and waiting for his hand to make contact with my flesh is thrilling and torturous. Even though his touch is not the one I crave, I still want to feel the contact of another while everything is so much more intense. The moment stretches out for long beats of time, but I feel nothing. Disappointment settles inside of me. I guess it is too much to ask for. I open my eyes to see Levi's hand wrapping around Jake's wrist, preventing him from closing the distance.

"Keep your hands off the angel," Levi growls.

Startled, I mist back through the wall. Both men swiftly follow me out.

CHAPTER 6

"You can both see me? Oh my!" I panic as I pace—about to go back to my cloud. This is too much for me to handle. Marcus is right. If the Council finds out about this, my grace will be taken. I am not supposed to be seen.

Sensing I am about to leave, Levi quickly closes the distance, wrapping his hand around my wrist. Everything comes to a halt for me. A terrible tightness forms in my chest from holding my breath, and a shiver rakes my body all the way to the tips of my wings. I guess I *can* feel touch in this state, and it is *electric*. I watch Levi's face go slack. Calmness suddenly radiates from him. Jake tilts his head to the side.

"The doors are locked if you would like to go

human for a little while," Jake says while walking to the door to double check the locks.

I look at Levi's strong, masculine hand still wraps around my wrist. He notices how my gaze lingers there and let's go. *I might as well just be corporal. They can already see me.*

I let myself come fully in, no longer misting between the worlds as a ghost would. The vibrant white of my peplo gown seems to glow against the pale perfection of my skin. I am suddenly self-conscious as to what he might think of my appearance. Nervously I run a hand over my hair with one hand.

Jake is all smiles except for the small pain in his eyes. I'm sure this comes from missing home. Levi studies me abstractly as if I am more of a puzzle and not a female. I find it disappointing and begin to wonder if it is my small breasts or my unshapely hips. The self-conscious feelings make me turn waspish toward him.

"Why have you been following me these past weeks?" Levi hisses.

I am caught off guard by his crude behavior. "I do *not* have to answer to *you.*" *The nerve of him, speaking to me like I am beneath him.*

"If you're going to constantly be on my ass, I want to know what the fuck for."

"How dare you talk to me in this manner?" I snap back at him.

Our voices compete for dominance over the other in snarling tones.

"I will speak any damn way I want. I've done nothing to warrant a visitation from you winged fucks."

"Well, I…" I cannot take any more of this. Upset, I mist out of the building completely. *Anger, this is anger.* I have never felt it this intensely. The urge to strike out and inflict harm is like fire in the veins and a gnawing in my gut.

Frustrated, I begin pace the alleyway, my white-blonde hair flying around me in total disarray. The smell of rotting food and urine is an ugly backdrop, matching the way I feel.

How can he be so...mean? Here I am, trying to make sure the Enforcers do not get called in to smite him, and he wants to be...an asshole. I stop my movements, shocked by my own choice of language—even if it is only in my thoughts.

Oh Deity, forgive me for using such language.

"Ugh!" I mutter loudly and strike my fist into the wall. There is no other word fitting enough to encompass his behavior. Pieces of brick and mortar crumble under the impact and fall to the ground. It feels good finding a physical release for my frustration.

I press my forehead against the wall. Its rough texture is not pleasant, but it grounds me. My hair falls forward, glowing in the dark of the night and acting as a curtain to block the world out. The uncomfortable pain makes me feel something other than the anger simmering inside. It was silly to entertain fantasies of showing myself to him when he feels this way toward my people.

I pictured myself going fully corporal, and him being awed by my angelic presence when I appeared. Levi would have slowly walked up to me, laying his hand upon my cheek as he leaned in and pressed his lips to mine.

Ha! It is a very laughable concept now. Thinking of it makes me wistful. Right now, I much rather leave him to the fate of another Watcher so I can get past these imaginings and back to my peaceful existence. Mind made up, I close my eyes and think of home.

Leaving becomes impossible when I am suddenly and forcefully pressed against the wall, my wings held down against my body. The arms wrapping in a vice around me belong to Levi. My wings give me added strength and having them immobilized leaves me helpless. I take a deep breath, readying myself to combat him—to show him I am no docile being. His scent filters in through the grime of the alley, and it angers me that I enjoy the light musky smell of it.

"You will answer me. I want to know why you have been following me." He leans harder into my body, the wall now scraping my cheek. "Is what Jake was saying the truth? Have you been sent to pass judgment on me?" He pushes harder, making me grunt from the pressure. "Tell me," he growls.

Finished with his line of questioning, I use every ounce of power at my disposal and snap my head back into his face. I feel a crunch and turn around as he lets me go.

"Mother. Fuck!" he says in a muffled voice while he holds his nose, blood trickling out steadily. "Whoever said angels are gentle were liars." He feels around his nose, ensuring it is not broken. Even if it is, he will heal as quickly as if it never happened—which is a plus side to being a half-breed.

He lifts the hem of his shirt and wipes his face, smearing the blood onto his chiseled cheek bones. I look down and find myself staring at the tan muscled plains of his chest, wondering what it would feel like to sink my nails into his flesh and hold on while he moves above me. The thought is completely wanton, and the sound of Levi clearing his throat brings me back from that dangerous thought. I look away, embarrassed to be caught ogling him.

I speak low but with superiority, knowing it will hit a nerve with him. "You have no right to manhandle me and expect me to answer your questions."

"But you can follow me around? Run and tell some fairy-ass-angel that it's time to kill me, for what, existing?" His voice is rising and so is my ire.

"That is not my job at all!"

"Well, then, what is it?" Levi's voice is deep and seductive even in his fury. It acts as fuel to the fire of my anger and excites me.

"I watch! That is all. I just watch."

"How long have you been watching me?"

The answer will upset him further, I am sure.

"What does it matter?" I snap back at him, growing more and more impatient with this conversation and not wanting to see anymore anger in his gilded eyes.

"How long?" Levi asks again.

Deity! The man is unrelenting.

I sigh deeply and close my eyes, not wanting to get lost any deeper in his golden gaze. "For twenty human years."

He is quiet for a long moment, so I open my eyes to find him staring at me fiercely and standing mere inches away. Even though he is angry, being this close to Levi makes me want to throw myself at him just so I can feel his touch once more but in much more personal places.

"Why come here now?" His voice softens and becomes more melodic and entrancing.

I almost want to give in and answer when he places his hands against the wall on either side of my head. How will he take it if I tell him I came here to be close to him? That he is my temptation, and I am testing myself. He will probably laugh at me.

Defiant to his request, I turn my head refusing to answer.

"Have you been able to see me this whole time?" I whisper. I try to be strong and look back into his lion-like eyes. Levi leans in slightly, and the need to crush my lips to his is so much more poignant the closer he comes to me, even with the blood smear still on his face.

"Yes. Are you going to answer me?" he asks.

Levi's voice becomes more coaxing in tone. He

rubs his cheek against mine. The stubble on his face causes goose-bumps to break out on my skin.

He slides closer to my ear and asks, "Why have you come to watch me this closely?" He pulls his face back just inches away now, and his breath flows against my lips.

My body is strung taut by nervousness. My nipples bead, practically begging for attention. and my peplo gown is unable to hide the evidence of it. I don't know whether to run away or close the gap between us. I choose the much easier path as he focuses on my lips. I mist away, thinking of only one place, home.

The cool fluffiness of my cloud touches my feet and I sigh. An awkward mix of emotions passes over me. Part of me is desperate for his touch. My heart is still racing from what contact I had.

How dare he treat me like a plague and then look at me with heat in his golden eyes. What am I going to do?

He is probably cursing me and my brethren. I want to look down on him to see his reaction.. An unsettling weight in the pit of my stomach has my sight zoning in on him now. I just have to know.

"Shit!" he shouts, and it echoes through the alley, scaring some stray cat into giving a yelp. He tugs his jeans trying to re-arrange himself.

I blush furiously as I notice he is hard, and the crown of his sex peeks over the waist-band of his jeans, making me want to reach out and slide my finger over the head of his member.

"I should've grabbed her," he mumbles under his breath while walking to the door of his bar. The neon lights from the sign saying Hell's Gates, casts an eerie light against the harsh lines of his face, making the smears of blood look black. I feel bad for a moment, but then I remember he had me pressed against a wall and vulnerable. Well, at least that is how I am going to justify it to myself. Plus, I am pretty sure the erection he has now is from the pain of his nose being busted and not from being pressed against me.

CHAPTER 7

"Where is Celine?" Jake asks and worry for me leaks from his voice.

I wonder if I knew him once. Unnerving is the best I can do to describe the idea that Jake has memory of me and I have none of him, if that is the reason he seems to care. It makes me wonder why became a Fallen all the more.

"How do you know her name, but she knows nothing about you? And how in the hell did I not know you are a fallen angel? Is your name even Jake?" Levi's ire is evidenced in his escalating smart-mouth tone.

"My name is Jacob, and it is none of your damn business why I am a Fallen. Now, where the fuck did Celine go?"

He says the last part mostly to himself, but Levi decides to put his own opinion in.

"I don't know. She just disappeared, probably to tell some higher up that I need to die now rather than later." He shrugs his shoulders trying to play it off, but it worries him, or he would not have assaulted me in the alley.

Maybe assault is too harsh a word since he was the one to leave the encounter bleeding and not I.

Ha! Teaches him not to under-estimate me.

"Figures her name would be Celine, Latin for Heaven."

He licks his lips, and my breath catches as he pulls his bottom lip between his teeth.

"She probably went back home." Jake takes a deep breath and looks at Levi. "You were too hard on her. Why wouldn't you let me touch her?" he asks with an attractive smirk as he throws a wet cloth at Levi, who uses it to wipe the blood off his hands and face.

"I was too hard on her? We are talking about my soul. I work too damn hard to stay out of hell for her to pass judgment on me. To tell some heavenly bureaucrat I'm not fit for heaven. Where the hell is the justice in that?" Levi sounds like a petulant child; one that is in need of a spanking. Like the ones he gives others.

The vision of him bent over to receive a spanking is quite laughable, considering his predilection for being the dominant male. Tantrum-like tone aside, the man has it all wrong. I am not going to correct him either. To correct him will be to tell him the truth.

Why did he disregard Jake's question about touching me?

"Did she say she was going to do that?" Jakes growing impatience makes him twist the towel that was over his shoulder in his hands.

"No, but she didn't say she wasn't going to do it either," he scoffs, not believing Jake.

I wish I could remember Jake. I wonder if he was a Watcher or a Joy Bringer. Enforcers rarely fall and are extremely easy to spot with their stature being as large as it is.

"Look man, Celine is... Well, she is..."

"She is what?" Levi asks throwing the cloth back at Jake.

He dodges the towel, and it makes impact with the colorful liquor-filled bottles lining the mirror behind the bar. Levi cringes as the bottles clatter against one another. I assume he hopes they do not break. Would serve him right if they did.

"She is naive. Celine doesn't understand the politics of The Council and isn't high enough in Watcher ranks to see the serious shit. I wonder why she is assigned to your ass."

How dare he! Naïve, he calls me. Well, I'm not the fallen one. I am assigned to Levi because I'm good at my job. Why is everyone so set against me being his Watcher? Okay, maybe I did slip in going to the earthly plane, but I had no idea that a fallen and a half-breed could see me. It is not like they have a handbook for this situation.

"I just want it to stop. She has been watching me for twenty fucking years." He sounds so disgusted.

The hurt blooms rapidly inside me. I clutch a hand to my chest, trying to combat the sharp ache.

Jake grunts at Levi. "Twenty? She hasn't been assigned for too long, so stop whining about it."

"That's almost two-thirds of my life, man! It's an invasion."

The longer I listen to Levi, the more foolish I feel for being so enamored with him. He despises my kind.

"Time works the same in Heaven and Hell, Levi."

"So…she has only been watching me for two years?"

"Yes, not like you can stop the nosey bastards," Jake scoffs.

I now wish I would have headbutted him as well.

"Well, it's two years too long," Levi whines.

"It's what she was created for. To watch is her calling." Jake shrugs, but he is right.

I am a Watcher. It *is* what I do.

"Listening to you and her talk about smiting me and shit was like a fucking solid hit to the gut." Levi shakes his head, struggling to finish his thought. "It's another damn reminder that heaven isn't going to want me. I'm just biding my time here until I punch out of life. Then, I'll be saying, 'Welcome to my joint in hell! Don't mind the blood, it brings a little color to the place,' in no time at all." He throws out his arm, mimicking showing his place off.

He is such a brat!

"I think she is here for another purpose, and if it's for what I think it might be…it's even worse than you being thrown into hell by the Enforcers." He looks thoughtful, rubbing the attractive stubble on his chin.

Does Jake really know? He must…with the way he looks at me and the almost touch of his hand on my face. He surmised my intentions before I was able to voice them myself. I wonder for the hundredth time who Jake is exactly. An even better question is, who was he.

"This is so fucked up…. I actually didn't mind her

being around. It gave me some kind of hope. I know now it was a false hope, but it was…comforting." He pushes his hair back from his face.

The look of defeat in his golden eyes makes my soul ache.

Levi mumbles, "I sound like a little bitch."

"You really do," Jake says, laughing.

"Fuck you, man. I should be mad at you too. This entire God-damned time we've known each other, you say nothing," he says with a snarky smile on his face.

"For not telling you what? That I am a Fallen? That you are being monitored by Angel Watchers? I came in here because *you* had an ad in the paper looking for help. It was coincidental that I'm an ex-angel and you're a half-breed."

"How can you tell I'm a half-breed?" Levi asks.

"I knew who you were before my fall. I didn't realize it was *you* until I walked in."

"Am I on some blacklist?" He closes his eyes and leans back in his chair. His hands rise to his face, and he rubs, forgetting I cracked him there earlier and wincing.

"You are the son of a high demon. Of course, you are watched."

"Watched by everyone or just by Celine? You

know what? I don't care. They need to just stop." His expressions and tone of voice when talking about me are just too saddening.

I can listen to his animosity towards my people no more. I open my eyes to look at endless fields of mist and white. I begin to will my cloud into changing shape. I picture the park I passed by daily while following Levi.

The picture is vivid, but the feel is not the same. The grass under my feet is still the cool fluffiness of my cloud. I lean against a tree, and the rough feel of the bark is not there to be abrasive against my skin. Just cool mist envelops me.

Stupid earthly plane, making me crave its textures and feel. The sensation of touch is so much more magnified, and I already yearn for it. I wrap my arms around myself, and the feel of Levi's touch is still seared into my skin. The warmth of his strong arms wrapping tightly around me and his deep voice speaking right next to my ear and vibrating against my back make me go weak-kneed. How can I want someone who despises what I am? Why would I jeopardize my calling and my grace for a touch?

Do your job, Celine. Just do your job.

CHAPTER 8

I wait the equivalent to one day on Earth to collect myself before heading back to the mortal plane. After the last encounter with Levi, I want to go into the situation with my rehearsed words and then swiftly remove myself from his presence. I also use this time to be completely honest with myself. I want to go back because I want to be near him one last time. If what they say is true, and admitting the problem is half the battle, then I am almost there. Being in his presence is addictive, and I swear curiosity will be my downfall and the loss of my wings.

I want to stop by and see Marcus before I leave. He put a mental call out to me twice since I made the transition back here to the heavens. I know he worries for my well-being, but he will ask why I am back so soon, and to answer him will be humiliating. I do not want to disappoint him any further. Although, I have a feeling he is sneaking peeks at what I am doing anyway.

I close my eyes and focus on Levi's soul signature. It is a little more difficult to transverse across without Marcus's assistance. As I arrive, I am automatically assaulted by metallic fumes. Breathing it in is thick and acidic on the tongue, with an edge of sweetness I cannot place. I look around and see I am in a darkened corner of Levi's garage.

The front end of a cobalt blue car faces the opened garage door. It has a ramp under each of the front tiers. Cinder blocks sit behind the back tires, and I assume it's to keep the car from rolling off and crushing the person underneath. Levi's legs stick out from under the vehicle. He has on his big, black motorcycle boots and those soft-looking worn jeans I have come to learn encase him perfectly. On closer inspection, I notice this is the vehicle I have seen Jake arrive in for work several times. For a moment, I wonder if he is close by.

Suddenly, Levi comes rolling out, a container of sloshing, inky black liquid in his hand. His hair is pulled back from his face, and I trace every line from his strong jaw to his hairline. I drink in his appearance and his presence, wanting to savor all before I leave for the safety of my home.

It is for the best, I tell myself. Knowing he could have reached out and touched me at any time makes me a tad nervous about my safety. The fact he didn't is both a relief to keeping my Angel status and a disappointment to the feminine part of me that craves him doing so.

He looks directly at me. No sunglasses to hinder my view of his gilded eyes. So, provocative with a touch of feral intensity. There is no more pretending he cannot see me. To demonstrate this, he stares at me head-on. I decide it couldn't hurt to be fully corporal here in the shaded corner of his garage. When I complete the full transition, I can feel his gaze, and it is almost tangible. His eyes trace over the lines of my face and body. Under his thorough scrutiny, I feel exposed—even more so with this encounter than the last. I work hard not to twist my gown in my fist. Especially since fidgeting is a sign of nervousness, and I do not need him to have that kind of power over me.

I rehearse in my head exactly what I want to say to him right now. To tell him how he is wrong about why I am here. That I will disappear back to my home, and he will no longer have to endure my presence in his life. No need for him to go through the rest of the time he has here on this mortal plane in paranoia that he will be snatched up and sent to hell. As long as he keeps to his current path, he will see the undying fields and be welcomed into heaven with open arms.

I try to open my mouth to speak, but the words are catch in my throat, a hard lump unable to move. I cough to clear this foreign sensation, but no relief comes.

"So, what brings you back to good ole Tess, Oregon? Is it the small-town life? Maybe the scenic views? Oh, no. I am sure you are here to spy on me some more. Need some new gossip for the office. Does the subject of my eternal resting place make for good watercooler talk?" His tone is sarcastic.

Suddenly, I do not want to reassure him anymore.

"Tess, Oregon is quaint and small-town life is just that, small. The ocean is quite breathtaking, and I have seen its views from the beach you tend to frequent often. Besides you are barely a footnote compared to the length of time I have been alive and will be just one more chapter I'll be moving on from. Your everyday happenings are inconsequential, and

I've no need to share its small existence with my Brethren." My tone makes me sound as if I am taking a lackadaisical approach to how he has to live his life, and it feels dangerously pleasant to be a little petty.

Once the words are out though, I ashamed the left my lips.

Is my pettiness a form of wrath? A type of vengeance in response to his behavior, and if that's the case, I am looking at three sins—all in the name of spending more time with Levi.

The look in his eyes goes from sour to extremely feral. Before I can catch a breath, he stands. The pan of oil is set off to the side with incomprehensible speed. His body seems to swell as he stalks toward me. I am once again struck by his masculine beauty. He reminds me of the feeling I get when I watch the day give way to the night. When the coming dark fades out the daylight, and I don't know if I should run for the shelter of the light or let the darkness consume me with its mysteries.

I happen to fancy what tales the dark likes to keep hidden.

Curiosity wins again as he walks toward me. Will he be angry enough to strike me? I know for sure he would never, but there is always that little bit of deviltry in him that makes me want to know what pleasure I can find in the pain he usually inflicts on others.

I shiver and remind myself this is still the man who helps little old ladies cross the road and loads groceries into their car. He is the man who helped mend a baby bird's wing when it fell out of a nest and the mother was nowhere to be found. My heart still melts when I think of the time and care he gave the bird. How he named the babe Blue, for he was a blue bird. Nourishing the little one until he could be out on his own. This is the man who shed a tear as he stood in awe of Blue flying his way to a freedom Levi probably wishes he can one day have.

Half way through his short journey to the corner where I stand, he pauses for a moment. A smirk graces his face. That side tilt of his lips makes me much more nervous than his feral look does.

Safe from the prying eyes of any humans who may be walking by, I remain in the same spot. I feel exposed to his stare and blurt out the first thought to come to mind.

"So, you are working on Jake's car? Is he nearby? I want to ask him a few questions."

He stops mid-step once again. "Do you think you

need him here as a buffer?" he says with and obvious irritation.

I wonder why. Unless he thinks I will harass his friend. Which he may be correct about.

I almost answer a resounding yes, but instead, I say, "No, not at all. I can take care of myself. Thank you, or do I need to remind you of who bloodied your nose in our last confrontation?"

Ha! Take that! I think to myself. I can hold my own against him. *I think...*

"So, you came here today to what, make me bleed again?" he says while taking the last couple of steps closer to me. "You watch me, so you must know how much I get off on pain. My pain and the other person's pain. An aphrodisiac for a demon half-breed like me. So, sugar, the only thing you did was give me a bit of foreplay." His voice turns deep and coaxing, no longer sarcastic.

Which is even worse because something deep within me begins to bloom in his presence. A gnawing ache to be one with him in some way, it is absolutely thrilling and excruciating, and I do not know how much more of this I can take.

He stands right in front of me. A hairsbreadth away, and I can smell his scent under the layers of sweat and grease from working on Jake's car. My knees go a little wobbly on me, and I work to keep my stance. This time, I let my hands curl into my gown rather than let them do what they are aching to do. Which is to grip onto Levi and pull him forward that last little bit. To feel his body against mine.

I want to close my eyes. Hide from him in some way. Maybe if I did, I can pretend this is not happening right now. I am so afraid of my body betraying me, but worse, I fear he will notice the affect he has on me just by standing so close. The tight knot in the center of me seems to unfurl in his presence. Tiny sparks of need flash through my veins. My breath quickens until I can no longer release the air and just hold it inside.

Levi reaches forward. In his golden eyes is a gleam of mischievousness. I shiver in anticipation, but he bypasses touching me completely to grab something behind me. I release the breath I was holding as he pulls back, a dirty blue cloth in hand. He doesn't move far enough away to give me space. The distance between us is too intimate for my comfort.

There is a childlike mirth in his eyes. I do not know if I should be offended or plain mad and embarrassment courses through me. I ignore it all though as another emotion flows in. Desire. It makes me hunger for things I know the mechanics of but have never engaged in. As my emerald eyes collide with the gold of his, I am grounded in this moment of quiet yearning.

"What really brings you back here, sugar? Now that I admit to being able to see you. I figure heaven is a much more suitable place for a being with your naivety. Are you here to spy on me, or…are you only back here to pump Jake for information?"

That irritated tone is back in his voice, and I mourn the loss of his sultry sound but figure it is good fortune. I have no idea how I will react should he aim those wiles at me and truly want to follow through with what his eyes seem to promise.

When his words fully penetrate this foggy state of mind I am overcome with something I cannot describe—other than it is like frustration of some sort. This emotion is about to erupt all over him if his condescending attitude does not let up. I've no idea what has come over me, but I close the distance between him and I. To do what, I have no idea, but his hands band around my arms and his grip is tight. So tight it borders on too much when his lips crash down upon mine. It is brutal and punishing, and I push into the contact, feeling the slight slice of his teeth from the pressure I added. He groans against me, and I gasp. The He uses the opening to thrust his tongue into me. He leaves no room for me to escape.

All I can do is take his ownership of my mouth and what air he deems to give. He takes possession of through his kiss making moisture pool between my thighs. I grow weak kneed——no longer able to withstand the sensual assault on my senses. He supports my body with his own, and out of nowhere, he pulls away. I fall to lean against the corner where I had been originally standing. He breathes heavily, chest rising and falling in rapid succession. The look in his eyes is molten. All of that gilded brilliance being focused on me is hypnotic.

The sound of footsteps shuffling closer startles me. I fade out of reality so as to observe and not be observed in the off chance it is a random human walking in. Jake walks into the garage, and his eyes move over Levi questioningly until they meet mine. I give up the pretense that I can hide. A smile breaks out over his face, and it is like the sun shining— warm and nourishing. I want nothing more than to embrace him like an old friend who has come back after a long absence. The feeling is beautiful and seems to grow the more I am in his presence.

I move toward him. He seems to want to do the

same. When I look over at Levi his face is blank, and he clears his throat before saying Jake's name.

Jake turns to the sound of Levi's voice and has his car keys tossed to him.

"Your car is ready. Help me get it off the ramp."

He looks at me, and the heat that blazed in his eyes is gone. It is now a cold look, and I feel everything that was blossoming inside of me shrivel in sadness at such a loss. My breath catches, and before I can release it, his voice breaks through with a harshness that grates against me.

"I'm sure you have other people to stalk and condemn. You should go play with them."

The words are like a slap to the face, but I still didn't say what I need to.

Looks like he is going to get his wish because, for the moment, I cannot stand to look at him. I mist back home once again, and I feel like a coward. I need to stay away for a few days and just watch from afar. It is what's best.

A couple of days pass until I am ready to look in on Levi. I need this time away from him. Our last encounter has seared its way into my being. I find myself with my fingertips pressing to my lips as I remember the feel of his tight hold on me. The crush of his mouth against mine. The slight coppery tang of blood where his teeth nipped at my lips. The way he sounded when he registered the slight sting of my pain.

I remember much more keenly how quickly it all came to a halt as Jake walked into the garage. Me, looking disheveled and a little embarrassed, and Levi, looking defiant and maybe even a little annoyed at the Fallen's presence. The habit of running away every time I am faced with these unfamiliar emotions is steadily wearing on me. Levi probably thinks me a coward, and I am pretty sure I am proving him right.

Which brings me to what I am doing to pass the time in a vain attempt at distraction. I spend almost all of it in the heavenly libraries looking for information. I was hoping for something I can access on Jake, but I find nothing. My hands graze over the leather-bound books that automatically fill in a soul's life as they live it. I try to feel for Jake's newly human life. It has been my only mission since returning home to take a small break from watching Levi.

My curious nature drives me to learn the reason Jake has become Fallen. Is his life of working in a bar worth it for him? This question plagues me. I seem to obsess over the idea of giving up our Deity's gift of immortality for only a handful of mortal years. And for what? Love, companionship, and even sex can be found here amongst our kind, should two beings feel a mutual inclination.

Though many of us do not travel down that path, already feeling fulfilled in our callings. Then again, I never questioned this possibility in all my years, not until Levi. To knowing there is a Fallen that can see me and who I can actually speak to lights my imagination on fire with many scenarios. I am positive not being able to see into his past is the gasoline on this burning curiosity.

The overwhelming feeling of familiarity I seem to share with Jake is just as harsh on my psyche. There is an intimacy, and it is just out of reach in the corner of my mind. It's there, this knowledge, and it almost works as the distraction I need from my ridiculous fixation on Levi. With all the searching, I locate nothing on Jake and decide to momentarily move on from this endeavor.

Why is there not a single word written anywhere? There is one section of the libraries we are not privy to. I stand, staring at the golden doors and wanting to step through them. Only one of The Council can enter them. The Fallen life records must be kept in there. What truly stumps me is why, through all the years of my existence, do I just now wonder about the Fallen life line. Of course, they are in the one place I cannot transverse without incur-ring The Council's wrath. A risk I almost want to take but will not.

I stand at the archway of the Soul Library and think of my dear Marcus. I must see him before I go home to my cloud. I am ashamed to admit to myself that, while I was in the human realm, I did not spare him a thought or two. I want to blame all the new sensations I was surrounded by, although I am pretty sure it is a very lacking excuse.

I smile as I recall the feeling of the sun warming my body while the wind whispers through my wings. Well, maybe it is a good reason after all. I shake the memory of sensation away and concentrate on thoughts of Marcus. I am instantly in his home. The foyer in which his cloud projects acts as a landing pad, not letting me in any farther unless he allows it. Not that I would barge in on him, but I can feel a barrier that was never in all my present before. It stings my heart a little for reasons I cannot grasp.

"Marcus, I am stopping by to say hello," I call. Hopefully, my presence assures him I am healthy and whole.

Marcus walks out, and his face glows with happiness. Now, why can't Levi feel the same?

I want to throw my arms around his broad shoulders and hold him so tightly he has to work to extricate himself from my grasp. His love always is a balm to my soul. I feel lighter being in his presence as if all the confusion weighing me down simply washes away in one glance. He is so handsome, I am sure if any human were to lay their sight upon him, they may cry.

"What brings you back to the heavens?" he says with a slight smirk.

I tense at his question his composure shifts.

"Did something happen on the earthly plane?" His face creases in lines of worry as he speaks.

Now, the glowing feeling starts to dissipate.

He is never this way about any other person I watch—only Levi. Why he worries is beyond my understanding. I smile and lightly clutch his arm in my hand. He wraps his hand around mine, keeping it against his skin. His hand is larger than mine, enveloping my own in warmth and comfort. Our eyes meet, and a question lingers in his gaze— one I do not understand. A piece of me feels like it might be vital to understanding why he has been behaving so protectively toward me.

Instead of asking the question, I let cowardice guide me and gently pull away from him. His entire demeanor changes with the distance. He stands to his full height. Marcus's eyes look on me, penetrative, and I want to confess everything to him in that moment. Instead, I say nothing to incriminate myself. For all I know, he would run to the Council himself just to have me removed from Levi. Even if it would be an easier course, I would rather do it in my own way, in my own time.

"I miss my home and want to feel my cloud under my feet after being gone for weeks," I say as straight faced as possible. Once again, the lies are bitter on my tongue, but I'm teaching myself to choke the taste down.

His quicksilver eyes swirl with a hypnotic quality, beckoning me to fall into their depth.

Marcus reaches a hand out to grasp my shoulder. "I am here for you, Celine. No matter the issue."

His grip tightens for a moment longer. I want to give in, and spill every last detail to him, but he releases me. I shake myself from his thrall. "I know, Marcus, and I thank you for your kindness and friendship."

"Why does that statement make me feel unsure? It feels more like you are saying farewell in a much more permanent way."

I clutch my gown in my hand and stiffen. Is that what I am doing? Surely not, but does he have a point? I fling my arms around him.

"You are being silly. I must go now." I leave him with that goodbye and mist out as quickly as possible.

In my home, I can feel my gown flutter where my heart is trying its hardest to beat out of its cavity. Levi swarms my thoughts as I lie on the floor of my cloud. Palms sweaty, I wipe them against the fabric covering my thighs. I breathe deeply in and slowly push the air from my lungs to calm the beating of my heart. It still races from my encounter with Marcus.

I will my cloud to make a mirror. It appears above me, and I look into its glassy reflection. Running a hand over my white blonde hair, I speak firmly to myself.

"You can do this, Celine. You are strong and capable." The affirmation has done little to calm my nerves, but still I chant it like it is the only life raft to be seen in the vastness of my existence. So melodramatic, and yet so true.

I continue to stare into the mirror self-consciously, getting lost in my reflection for a moment. My eyes are dilated so that only a rim of their usual emerald green is showing. A pink tint colors the apples of my usually pale cheeks. I begin to compare myself to the other women I have seen Levi with and swipe at the misty mirror. I was not made his Watcher to ogle or to be ogled by him in return. I am his Watcher because his soul is at stake, and that above all else is my priority.

CHAPTER 10

Concentrating the coolness surrounding me and seeping into my feathers, I let my sight take over and zone in on Levi. My heart is beating furiously. I wrap my arms around my stomach while it twists in pretzel-like knots. I see him in his house. It's a modest dwelling. Furniture is sparse, and his cream-colored walls are empty. A blank canvas he does not fill but for the windows that hang with sheer curtains. Levi enjoys wide open spaces. I have heard him call himself a minimalist. I call him claustrophobic, stemming from his fear of being trapped in hell alongside Malacoda.

Levi owns a large television, and I have seen him waste away days at a time, getting lost in movie after movie. I wonder if, while I was away and not watching him, Levi enjoyed the company of another female. Did he take them to his special room at the members-only club? The thought has my chest constricting my lungs and my hands balling into fists. Why this possessiveness over him, when before, I would have secretly enjoyed the small glimpse of his passion?

I find him in his living room. Slouching on the plush black suede sofa. He wears only a pair of jeans only, feet bare and a bottle of what looks like bourbon in his hand. The dragon tattoo on his arm gives the illusion of movement as he raises the bottle to his lips. Levi's body stiffens, and he stops just before his mouth makes contact with the glass rim.

"Come out, come out wherever you are," he says in a sing-song tone. Levi takes a substantial pull from the bottle in his hand and sucks a breath in between his teeth. The amber liquid sloshes around its glass casing. "I can *feel* you *watching* me." He closes his eyes and tilts his head back. "Are you too good to come say hi to the person you're looking to condemn to hell?"

He is goading me. I know this, but like a fool, I am going to go to him. I thought a few days away would help this affliction, but no. His pull on me is stronger now I have felt his touch. I'll damn myself for this later and give into the sinful temptation of his presence right now.

I find it easy to mist my way into this realm. I am focused as to not be bombarded with so much sensation that it is too disorienting. My breath catches in his presence. Being this close to him weakens me. All I can seem to do is remember how hard his body will feel against me if he pulls me close again. How his lips feel soft but unyielding. I almost whimper but try my hardest to compose myself for this confrontation.

I am too attached to him, and I know I desperately need to stay away.

Give him to another Watcher, my sense of self-preservation whispers.

All that is light and love inside me rebels against it. I truly want what is best for Levi. Seeing him cross over to this side of the veil and into the undying fields of heaven will make the ache of separation worth it. He can have a peaceful, heavenly life. One I cannot be part of, but it will be one of serenity and love. Though I know this to be true, the thought of him being completely out of my reach feels like sharp, burning stabs to the chest.

"Ah…there you are. Do you feel safer being around me as a pale outline?"

Levi's voice acts as a lure, bringing me to step closer until I am standing in front of him. His face is slightly scruffy, and his hair is a halo of black velvet—almost blending into the couch. He looks tired. Lines of worry are etched into his face.

"I will remind you again. I did not know you could see me at the time." I speak softly, not out of shyness, but in fear he will start berating me again and make me angry enough to strike out at him. Or worse, throw myself at him only to be rejected harshly.

"Do you always speak so damn politely? I feel like I need to sit up straighter the moment you start talking. I'm not going to, but the thought is there." He takes another swallow of his drink. The liquid swishes around as he brings the bottle back down to rest at his beautiful bare feet.

As Levi comes back up, he snatches my wrist. His grip is strong, and his touch creates a simmering heat deep inside me.

"Do you always have to be so negative?" I scold, becoming fully corporal. He already has me in his grasp, so I might as well enjoy the electrifying contact. Is this what it feels like to be an addict? Will

I always crave his touch above all else? Maybe even over my own grace. I am so exhausted from turning this question over and over in my mind.

"You were gone awhile. Did you find someone else to spy on? And, yes, I like being an asshole." He yanks on my wrist, making me fall forward onto him. I use my other hand to catch myself against his shoulder. My hair surrounds us like a curtain, providing an agonizingly intimate privacy. The moonlight streaming in catches the strands and makes, them glow, seeming to invite Levi to sift the strands through his fingers. As light as a butterfly's wing and as devastating as the storm brewing inside of me. I breathe Levi in deeply. The scent of his natural musk with the bite of alcohol is sinful.

"I did not say you are a… I *said* you are negative." My tone is shaky from being so close to him. My body has a slight tremor from balancing myself over him.

Levi brings his hand down from my hair, so slowly. He wraps it around my hip, and I feel the touch brand me. His fingers press firmly into my flesh. Pulling me forward, he uses his knee to wedge between my legs. My gown splits high up my thigh, exposing creamy pale skin. The hunger in his eyes make my breasts swell and nipples bead for more of his attention. This aching need is delicious, and it scares me to know just how much more I want.

"You can't say asshole, or do you choose not to have a potty mouth?" As Levi speaks, he raises his other hand to my face, and I rub myself into it like a kitten seeking affection. And, like a kitten, I want to purr. His barely callused hands against my soft skin are an erotic contrast. My wings flutter, and my body trembles. The electric current runs a path to my core and makes my sex slick with desire.

"I am respectful. A lesson you need to be taught," I whisper. Our lips are only a mere graze away from each other. The space is so sensually charged that strands of my hair begin to float. I can taste the liquor he consumed as our breaths mingle.

"I wonder if you will taste as sweet as you smell…."

His voice is like silk running over my body, willing my sex to dampen my thighs.

"What do I smell like?" I am shocked by my own sultry voice. I did not know it was in me to be sexy in any way. I can feel a change in me. My limbs are just a little more lax. The need for friction mounts with each second that passes. What kind of friction I have no idea, but the want for it is tantamount to something my body is searching for.

"Sugar cookies, warm out of the oven. The ones that melt in my mouth the moment they touch my tongue." Levi licks his lips, and they just barely graze mine.

"I...I..."

Levi closes the distance. His lips press against mine. I gasp and moan into his kiss. He licks my bottom lip, coaxing me for entrance into my mouth. This kiss is nothing like the first one we shared. This one is a slow exploration. Heat pouring from him into me, loosening my limbs. I melt into this slow burn. He tastes of liquor and some spice unique to him. His mouth on mine can only be described as wicked. So very bad, and I want to open more than just my mouth to his tongue. Where this thought comes from, I do not know, but I need.

I need so badly.

I've seen the act done between so many. People sacrifice their very livelihoods to obtain this sensual touch. Never once did I want to know what they were trying to achieve. At this very moment, all of my long life seems to have condensed down into the decision I will make here and now.

The only answer my body gives me is that I feel starved. A hunger like no other for the feel of him rides me. In this time and place, the feel of Levi in any way I can have him is the only service I want to be in. After two thousand years of wanting nothing but to be of service to *my* people and to guide souls from the brink of unending darkness I am ready.

I am empowered and a little lightheaded as I make my decision and give into him teasing my mouth.

"Mmm...you taste so fucking good," he says around nips and licks.

The stimulus is so intense my wings involuntarily pop open, startling him. He chuckles, making me feel self-conscious.

"Did I do something wrong?" I try to pull away as he continues to laugh, but he holds me tighter.

Levi pulls me into his lap more firmly. My legs straddle him. The sheerness of my gown is no real barrier to his heat. A heat that penetrates me to my core.

"You feel this?" he asks, pushing his groin up against me. "My cock does what your wings just did."

The hard length of him presses against my sex. I remember the peek I had of him when he cornered me in the alley and clench my hands in want.

My sex dampens, and he is only kissing me. A kiss, one that makes my blood boil. I finally get the courage to do something I dream of. I slide my fingers into his obsidian hair and tug his head back. I forget my strength and the action is more forceful than I intend.

"Ah, fuck." He groans against my mouth.

I whimper softly in return. My lips part as the feel of his soft locks in my hands excite me. I grip the strands tighter as Levi slides his tongue into my mouth, and I tentatively meet his with my own. I moan into his mouth. Our tongues dance, deep and slow against one another. I rock my body against his, gripping his shoulders as I help stoke this fire inside of me. Each grind of my hips sends a zinging sensation through my body, making my wings rise higher. His hands grip my hips while he pushes up against my sex.

"God, I can feel how hot your pussy is through our clothes."

His words are dirty and tantalizing at the same time, making me pant. I throw my head back and moan as the feeling of quickening spurs me on.

"I want you so damn bad, Celine. Seeing your pale outline everywhere I turn and trying not to touch every inch of you is excruciating." Levi's grip on me tightens. "All the places I dream of putting my hands and tongue." He groans while pushing up even harder against me.

His words act as an aphrodisiac to my rising lust, making me slicker with desire. Levi moves my hips in a push and pull manner as he guides me. He glides my hot, soaking-wet sex against the thin material of my gown. I am so close. My hands move back up to his hair. The inky strands are wrapped in the tight grip of my fingers, surely causing him pain.

"Oh, Levi, yes! Please don't stop. Yes!" The plea flows from my lips in desperation to finally succumb to the building passion he elicits in me.

"That's right, sugar. Beg me." He holds my hips still, and I try to fight it. Using all of my might to move against him, but he keeps me still.

"Please… Oh Deity, please…" I whimper. My orgasm being withheld after denying myself for so long is a sharp ache.

Levi reaches up and slips the shoulder straps of my gown down, exposing my small, pert breasts. I grind against him, trying to regain the momentum of my release. His hands cover my breasts, massaging them roughly. I cry out, arching my back, and my nipples bead for him.

Levi pulls me forward, looking me in the eyes while he fastens his lips around one of the budding protrusions and flicks his tongue around it. The sensation travels through my whole body, making my sex throb even harder. I grind against him forcefully now. His rigid length and the denim of his pants make the friction so much more intense.

"Where have you been, Celine?" he asks, holding my hips still once more. Levi sinks his teeth in, around my nipple—just shy of painful and making me yelp.

"I needed time to separate myself from you. Please, Levi," I let the truth slip from me quickly, in hopes he will start moving against me again. My hands grab his shoulders, nails digging into his smooth, tan flesh, and I tremble.

"I don't want you to leave me. Everything is empty when you're gone." He pulls my head down and crushes his lips to mine.

The slide of our tongues against one another and his declaration makes my soul soar and my body scream for more.

"Mmm… Yes, Levi. Please move against me." I beg with a moan.

"What were you doing while you were gone?"

His hands guiding my hips back and forth are paced tortuously slow. The realization he is using sex to interrogate me is a distant thought as it works its magic and loosens my tongue.

"I was looking for Jake." I barely get the words out before his grip changes from passionate to aggressive, fingers digging into my waist.

"Jake?" Anger passes quickly across his face. "Were you looking to have his touch again?" Levi's words are no longer smooth but gravelly. The demon in him pokes its head out to play. "Did you want him to touch you touch you? Here I spent the last two weeks wondering if you had forsaken me."

His growling vibrates against me, heating me up instead of making me run. *Do I have no self-preservation instincts?*

"I was actually missing your presence, and you were too busy chasing after the damn Fallen." I hear the rip of fabric as he uses one hand to tear at his jeans and the other to pull my gown open. The soft material floats down to pool around my waist. I try to tear my eyes away from his shaft

Seeing it in person is an experience in itself. He is thick and long. The slopped head of it beads a pearly liquid. I use my index finger to spread the warmth around. I lift the digit to my mouth and snake my tongue around my finger, savoring his unique flavor.

"Oh my fucking God, Celine."

He pants, and I feel sensual and strong to be bringing such a reaction out of his usually stoic self.

Levi's gaze is riveted to my body. His eyes travel over my breasts to my waist and settles at my bare sex. He licks his lips as if he can already imagine tasting me there, and it makes my core throb.

"You didn't answer me, Celine."

"No…I just want to know. Oh Deity!" I shout to the rafters as Levi's fingers start gliding through the wetness of my core, slowly rubbing at the bud of my sex with the moisture he collects.

"Know what, Celine? Did you want to know his touch? I stopped it from happening before, and I'll fucking do it again." He thrusts his finger into my wet channel meeting with my virginal barrier. He looks me in the eyes. His intense gaze fills with a predatory light.

Levi growls. "Mine!" Then, he thrusts two fingers fully inside of me.

My body stills from the pain, putting a damper on my lust. The sharp sting causes a few tears to trickle down my face. I knew it would hurt, but I never imagined it would be this painful.

"Oh, fuck!" he mutters. Levi's eyes roll as he tilts his head back. His pupils fully dilate, leaving the thinnest rimming of gold.

Oh Deity! He is feeding on my agony. The pain of my virginity is giving him sustenance. I am feeding a demon. I get up and move quickly away, my gown still held around my waist by a braided belt. I watch as he sits in his euphoria from causing me discomfort. *How could I do this to myself? My grace, my home, and my brethren could all be lost on someone who does not love me.* I pull my gown together and begin to mist away.

"Celine, please don't go," Levi calls, but it's too late.

The last things I hear are his cursing and the crash of what I assume is his bottle of liquor. My breath catches on a sob in my throat. This was not how it was supposed to go. All I wanted was a taste of sensation with the man who haunts all my fantasies. I am so enthralled with him, but it's not reciprocal and never will be.

What have I done?

I materialize in front of Levi's bar and see Jake locking the door. I watch him shiver, knowing it is from my presence and not the cool evening. He turns to look at me. Taking in my disheveled appearance, his eyes linger on the tracks of tears falling from my eyes. He wraps his arms around me. The peace and comfort coming from his embrace is immediate.

"Celine, are you calm enough to mist us both away?" Jake's voice is soothing as he calmly strokes my hair.

"Yes, I think so." I close my eyes and wait for the warm tingles of Jake's soul to brush against mine.

"Good. Now breathe and feel my intent. Can you

feel where I want to go?" His voice is a little shaky with the intimate experience.

"I can, yes." It is the feeling of home. The house will be in a small neighborhood where lawns are well manicured and a dog off in the distance barks in a deep bass tone,. That little extra bit of information makes me smile. I know how much the dog's barking annoys him now.

"Let's go," he says.

We mist away. As soon as we arrive, Jake releases me quickly. We materialize in front of a large wooden door. I stay as a shade, not knowing who may be around. I feel a couple of life presences beyond the door. Jake sticks his key inside the locking mechanism and turns. He pushes the large oak door open and walks in a couple of steps.

"Where are we?" I ask figuring it was his home but wanting to know for sure.

"This is my place. Please, no questions until the woman who is here leaves." He continues in and walks towards the large chair in the corner of the living area.

Pictures of a sweet child hang on the taupe colored walls. The furnishing is simple and comfortable looking. An elderly woman sits there peacefully asleep. A magazine sits across her ample bosom like a blanket, and a small bit of drool hangs from the corner of her mouth. Jake pats the little, old, silver-haired lady on the shoulder and speaks softly.

"Mrs. Davidson, time to wake up."

"Hey, Jake! You're home early," she says with a yawn. She squints at her watch and begins to stand, using Jake's hand for assistance.

I use my sight and flash on her life. A widow for the last ten years, she has lead a quiet life. No children because of an accident when she was young. Mrs. Elizabeth Anne Davidson lives next door to Jake and worries for him like the son she will never have. Mrs. Davidson even saves the money he pays her for watching his daughter Karina in an account that will go to Karina when she graduates high school.

A daughter... Amazing!

"Yeah, a friend dropped me off." He holds onto Mrs. Davidson's arm as they make their way to the front door. "How was Karina tonight?"

"She was a talkative little monster tonight." The words are harsh, but the smile on her face says otherwise. "She made me read the same book to her three times in a row before she would let me leave her side."

"I really don't know what I'd do without you.

Thank you for caring for her this evening." The gratitude pouring from Jake makes Mrs. Davidson beam in happiness.

"You're a sweet man, Jake. You must let me set you up on a date. I know the sweetest young woman." She pats him on the cheek, turns, and walks out of the door.

Jake stands there, watching as she walks towards her house. Only when her silhouette disappears completely from view does he come back in. I smile at him when the sweet sound of his child drifts closer to us.

"Daddy? Are you home, Daddy?" a groggy voice says as his daughter, Karina, steps into view. Her curly mahogany hair surrounds her and makes her sea green eyes stand out in beautiful contrast, just like her father's. She is petite and stands to about my hip.

"Hey, baby girl! You need to go to bed, sweetheart. Come on. I'll tuck you back in." I enjoy this interaction between the two of them. Jake is a father, and a good one from what I see of Karina's short life. Her mother is not present in any conscious memory but for one that is buried deep, and I cannot see it. Just the maternal vibrations come through.

"Can the angel tuck me in too?" She looks over

at me.

I'm shocked she can see me. Then again, she is half angel, so it would explain the sight.

"Of course. Celine, will you come with us?" Jake sighs and looks to me with pleading in his eyes. How could I resist the request of such a special child?

"I would be honored to."

We make our way down the hall, the hardwood floor creaking under their footing. I am still not fully corporal, so I pretty much glide along, soundlessly like a ghost.

"Why do you look so sad? Usually the angels I see smile a whole bunch more than you are right now." Even though she means no harm, her words sting me. I have not been truly happy in a long while, even before being assigned to Levi. I always feel like I am missing something important, or there is more for me out there somewhere.

"Celine has had a very trying night, sweetheart." Jake pulls the pretty purple comforter up to her chin.

Little hot air balloons are the main décor in the room with little paper angels scattered across the walls. It is whimsical and reminds me a little of heaven with the cotton ball clouds and the little paper people sitting in them.

"Is she going to stay with us now?" Karina asks

with a sleepy yawn. "Andy, the boy from class, has an angel who lives with him. He doesn't know it, and I didn't tell him, Daddy. I promise." She looks up at him with her sleepy, innocent eyes.

Yearning to share my life with another settles deep in my heart.

"No, baby, she is just visiting for a while. I am happy you didn't tell him. It's for his angel to let him know."

He is so patient with Karina. So opposite to how he is around Levi.

"Daddy, can you read to me?" The words barely leave her pretty cupids bow lips before her eyelids begin to flutter closed.

"I think Mrs. Davidson read to you plenty tonight. It's time for you to go back to slumberland." He leans down and lightly kisses her brow, smiling as he pulls away.

"I hope you feel better, Ms. Celine."

I smile at her, even knowing her eyes are closed, and she cannot see me.

"Thank you, Karina," I say softly as Jake and I leave the room. I make myself fully corporal as we walk back down the hallway, dragging my fingers against the wall. The flat paint is silky and chalky at the same time.

Jake motions me over to the camel colored suede sofa, much the same as Levi's. I tuck my wings in close to lie flat against my body, so I can sit back.

"Would you like something to drink?"

I begin to shake my head, but he puts a hand up to stop me.

"I know you don't need it, but I figure you might like to try it out." He smiles, knowing darn well the thought of experiencing anything while in this form is intense and welcome.

"I would love some. Thank you. Actually, do you have wine?" I might as well go for gusto. My feathers flutter in excitement.

"Are you sure?" Jake asks with a bit of trepidation in his voice.

"Yes. I am sure. I have always wanted to try it, and I seem to be all for trying new things these days." I will not let the censure in his voice put a damper on this new experience.

Jake disappears through a doorway to what I assume is the kitchen. A few moments later, he walks in with a glass of the deepest red liquid and the wine bottle in his other hand.

"Here you go. Sip it." He hands the glass to me by the stem. "Take your time. Savor it."

"Thank you." I take a small pull on the drink. It is

full-bodied with subtle spices of the land that grew flavorful in the grape. The complexity dances on my tongue. As I swallow a few more pulls of this decadent drink, my limbs grow heavy, and my tongue loosens.

"So…I assume Karina is part of the reason for your fall," I blurt out without caring that it might be a sensitive subject for him.

"She is, yes. Though I miss home and my brethren, I would give it up all over again in a heartbeat for her," he says, smiling at some far-off thought I would desperately like to know.

"She has your beautiful eyes," I say, leaning in to get a better look into the sea green depths.

"Thank you. Most days, I see her mother in her face." Sadness colors his tone.

I reach out to pat his shoulder but use a little more force than necessary. Jake winces and rubs the spot I was patting.

Whoops!

"Maddie, Karina's mother, was a pain in the ass, especially while she was pregnant." He smiles. "Her death was unexpected, but Karina and I have made a nice, quiet life for ourselves."

I smile and it makes me feel like laughing. *Wow, wine is like magic. I need more of this red miracle juice.*

"This makes me feel…giggly," I say, waving my glass at him for a refill.

"Want to tell me why you are so…" Jake asks, motioning towards my still disheveled appearance.

"Levi, of course," I say with a heavy sigh. Throwing my head back into the couch cushion, I allow images of his golden gaze and the feel of his hands and mouth on my body swim to the forefront. The sharp ache between my thighs forces my legs to close.

Jake clears his throat, and I come back to my senses.

"I let him…touch me."

"I see, and…"

He is baiting me for a full answer. The look on his face tells me he already knows what I have to say.

"I was a virgin, so it hurt. And he…he…" I couldn't even finish saying it. Feeding a demon and being with my charge sexually, for that matter, is not going to keep my grace. I am so going to lose my wings.

"He fed off the pain," Jake says, like it is no big deal.

He knows what I risk, and he treats it so nonchalantly.

"Oh Deity. Yes. I fed a demon. Me, an angel, fed a

demon," I say in exasperation. The wine makes me slur my words and speak in a belligerent tone. Not that I care at the moment.

"You know he feeds involuntary. Someone can stub their toe while he holds their hand, and Levi would get excited." Jake shrugs.

It makes me want to smack him. Just what a female wants to hear the man she wants would act that way towards anyone who endures bodily harm. *Jerk!*

"Well, that makes me feel special," I say punctuating it with a large hiccup and heavy emphasis on the 'S'.

"You are special to him, Celine. You should've seen him these past weeks. He was a damn moody mess." A small part of me is thrilled to hear that and wants desperately to believe I mean something to him in a way that is not sexual or a one-way ticket into hell. *Who in the hell am I trying to kid here?* All of me is thrilled and wants to believe in his feelings.

"With the way he treats me, you would think I was a plague. I have seen the plagues, so you cannot tell me otherwise." *Whew!* I am so hot and dizzy.

I start to fan myself, and Jake catches the glass from my hand as I tip over and feel the fibers of the sofa against my face.

I open my eyes when I hear a buzzing sound. Jake's silky voice lulls me to sleep. I close my eyes for what feels like a second. When I open them, I am greeted by the sound of Levi and Jake talking in low, aggressive tones. Jake shakes his head at Levi's back as he pushes his way in. Levi walks toward the sofa I have no intentions of vacating, and he just looks at me. He holds his body regally like a king. Levi is so strong and virile, but in his eyes, I see vulnerability. Is it fear that I will turn him away? Again.

Jake speaks softly. "You guys are both pretty fucked up. Stay in the spare room tonight." Levi nods and makes his way towards me.

I want to say no, but the closer he comes, the more whole I feel. I want his arms around me, holding me tightly and telling me he wants me as much as I want him. I am so pathetic.

Levi picks me up, and even in this drunken stupor, I am in awe of his strength. He carries me with such ease that we are practically gliding to the room on the other side of the house. Levi jostles me around while he tries to pull the sheet down on the bed. I feel the soft, yet firm, give of the mattress as he sets me down gently. I moan, luxuriating in the smooth cool sheets.

Levi strips down to nothing, and my feathers, flutter at the scintillating sight, despite being tucked in close to my body. Could the creator have made anyone more physically perfect? Smooth muscles stacked on his six-foot-two frame and a face to render you speechless in its masculine beauty. What really sets Levi apart from the rest is the power and raw magnetism he exudes.

Levi climbs into the bed beside me, reaches his arms out, and pulls me close. He kisses my forehead, and I melt into his embrace. In my drunken state, I am so confused. My emotions are cascading in unidentifiable patterns. Joy, sadness, excitement, fear, hope, pain, anger, and even love stream through me. A kaleidoscope of feelings I have never experienced in full, crash violently against my soul.

"I am so sorry, Celine. Please forgive me. I should've never taken your innocence away from you like that. I am sick because I fed from the pain. I know it's a lame excuse, but I can't control it."

Sincerity clings to his voice and makes me want to listen. I say nothing, only watch as the moonlight filters in, highlighting the stubble on his face. I glide my hand against his cheek, and he closes his eyes and nuzzles in. He is so desperate for a gentle touch that he is practically purring.

"I have to confess something to you."

Levi holds his breath as if preparing to tell me something I am sure will have me curling up in the fetal position.

"Are you seeing another angel?" I ask jokingly, hoping to defuse the tension. Well that, and I am pretty sure I'm drunk.

Levi's face gives no hint to what bomb he plans to drop on me. He looks so serious, even with his hooded bedroom eyes. I pull my hand away from his face, and I wait as patiently as I can for what he has to say.

"Celine, I have known about your presence for a long while. I didn't put it together until you came down and misted around me, but I always knew you were with me. You make me feel...complete and peaceful."

Levi's words make my feathers flutter excitedly, and I try to play it off by shifting around, hoping he does not notice. He is so loquacious when he has been drinking, and I like it. His hardened exterior and words are all for show, and his need for control and distancing himself from people makes him act brash. I have always understood the why, but to have the attitude pointed at me is painful.

"Sometimes, when I 'spied' on you," I say, putting my finger in those little bunny ears I see people do when quoting someone, "I would see you shiver when I focused too hard. I would almost slip between the veils separating us." I am also admitting things too freely. I need to think before I speak before I say something I cannot take back, like how the sheer curtain defuses the light and shines on him in a way that makes me want to rub myself all over him. Shaking my head, I try to ignore my inner musings and listen to him.

"When my mother passed away, everything

became so much harder for me. My hungers were threatening to turn me into the monster my father wants me to become." He reaches out for my hand, entwines our fingers, and softly strokes his thumb over mine.

"I want you close to me. When you are near, it is like being bathed in hope. When you are gone, I feel empty. Lost. This all sounds so selfish, saying it aloud," Levi mumbles, "but I need you."

I cut him off before he can continue.

"It is selfish, you baboon! I am a sweet and kind angel. You, sir, are an ass. Ha, I can say that word," I say playfully and slide closer to him, slipping my leg between his as we lie on our sides. The need to be as close as possible to Levi is driving me to shed my inhibitions further.

Levi smiles at my little tirade.

"When you came down to this plane, I watched you the best I could out of the corner of my eye. It was joyful, fucking joyful."

The goofy grin on his lips has my heart beating erratically.

"I caught you putting your hand under the bathroom faucet. The stream of water cascading over your fingers made your eyes sparkle. I swear, inner light exudes from you in your happiness, and it is breath taking."

"Wow! I am the worst Watcher ever. Here I am supposed to be keeping track of everyone and being all stealthy, but instead, they were all just blatantly watching me. The shame!" I dramatically put a hand to my forehead and giggle. *I am pretty sure I am supposed to be mad at him for something, or am I supposed to be mad at myself?*

"Not to mention seeing your full form had me digging my nails into the palms of my hands to stop myself from reaching out and touching you." Levi grips my hand a little firmer, bringing it up to his mouth to softly press a kiss to my knuckles.

The sweet contact sends little electric tingles traveling to some very choice areas of my body .

"I'm sorry for how I acted at the bar. When I heard you and Jake talking about smiting me, it was like every dream I pinned my hopes on about walking through the pearly gates and calling the clouds home were gone in the one minute of conversation you had with the damn Fallen."

He pauses for a moment, and I stare into Levi's haunting lion-like eyes. Even in the velvet dark of night, they are still vibrant in the moonlight. His gaze heats as he talks about my conversation with Jake, and I assume it's in anger and disappointment.

"I wasn't even going to let on that I knew you guys were talking about me, so I could keep you by my side. I thought if I acknowledged you were there, you would go away. And, of course, you did. But when I saw pretty boy about to put his hands on you and you willing and fucking anxious for Jake's touch, something in me snapped."

Oh my! He is growling and possessive, and I love the way it makes me feel.

"Levi, his touch was not the one I wanted, but I never imagined there would come a day that the person I wanted would even know I existed, let alone touch me." I yank my hand away from him and cover my mouth. *Holy Deity! Did I just say that out loud?*

Levi smirks, and I smack him lightly on the chest.

"I was an asshole. I couldn't bear the thought of you enjoying his hands on you. I want you, Celine."

The way he says my name makes it the most sensual sounding word ever said.

"I feel like you are the other half of what is missing from me. I'm not saying I know you, but something about you has my mind and body screaming, *'Mine.'* I'm wrecked when you're gone, Celine."

I hurt for him and myself, and without saying a word, I press my lips to his. Our tongues tangle in a slow, erotic dance—slipping and sliding against one another. We each compete for dominance over the other's mouth. The lingering taste of liquor on his breath is just as intoxicating as before.

Levi pushes me to lie flat on my back as his lips move away from mine, leaving a sizzling trail down my neck. He hovers over me, slowly moving down and biting around my breasts through the fabric. Then, he uncovers them by leisurely pulling the gossamer fabric to the sides. The cool air against the aching buds of my breasts sting in the most delicious way.

Levi licks his lips, and I writhe just a little in response. My hands clutch his smooth, muscular back. He puts his weight fully on top of me, pushing my thighs open wide with his knees. Levi drags my hands away and pins them above my head. I arch my back, relishing the feel of the beaded peaks rubbing against his hot flesh. His erection presses against the apex of my thighs, and subtly, I rock into him as he peppers kisses along my neck and up to the lobe of my ear.

"Will you let me do something for you, Celine?"

"Levi, I… Oh my! Please don't stop." I moan into his neck as he rocks against my sex.

He moves down, and the loss of him pushing against me makes me cry out. My head whips back and forth, my white-blonde hair flying in its wake. Levi leans up and unties the braided belt at my waist, opening the gown for his viewing pleasure.

I shiver at the hunger in his eyes and briefly wonder if he will give me pain with my pleasure. I've no idea how I feel about experiencing his particular brand of carnality. I tremble from the tip of my toes to the roots of my hair, vulnerable and exposed.

The pleasure he offers me comes with a price on my end. Is this feeling worth it? I ask this of myself over and over again. I have asked it for the last year of my life. Is this slow burn building inside me once more, worth it? I look into his eyes as he watches my reaction. The need burns brightly. Lust only barely banked. His restraint is etched in the tightening around his eyes and his sinfully full lips. Lips I dream of even in my waking hours.

"God made you so fucking perfect. I don't know where to start tasting you first." He moves farther down, licking and nipping his way towards my abdomen, over my hip, and down the side of my right thigh. Levi's hair trails across my sensitive body, making me shiver in pure ecstasy. His tongue licks up the inside of my thigh, and both my hands clench the bed sheet on either side of me.

I become self-conscious as I realize where his mouth is heading and try to close my thighs. What if I taste different, bad. I wouldn't know. I have never even touched myself in this way. I've not been inclined to. It is only recently this yearning for more, a touch not my own, consumes me. I will him to look at me once more. I need Levi to anchor me here in this moment, so I do not fear what I cannot change.

I watch his dark head rise, answering my unspoken call. His golden eyes are glowing with heat, and I am sure he would find the same fire has now been reignited in the green of mine. He lowers his head and flattens his tongue. Then, he gives my already wet sex one long lick from the opening of my core to the hardened bud.

My hands fist whatever bed coverings are beneath me. That one stroke of his tongue ignites a path of electric tingles through my entire being. My panting is shallow, and I cannot pull in a full breath. It makes me light headed and desperate for more of his mouth all over me.

"Your pussy tastes so good, baby." He moans into me, still working his tongue up and down. He gently sucks on the outer lips of my sex with a small audible pop, and I jump.

"Sweet heavens, Levi! Please, Oh Deity, don't stop. Ugh!" My moaning becomes disjointed, unrecognizable sounds.

Levi wraps his arms under and around my thighs to stop me from thrusting my pelvis erratically towards his mouth. He teases so spectacularly, and I can feel my quickening. I have never once imagined it could be so powerful, the build up to what promises to be a spectacular release. I feel a rising panic that I'll lose this sensation cresting to a full completion.

Oh Diety, please, please, please, I beg to myself.

Everything surrounding me fades away, and my vision is a blur of tears. Frustration takes over from being held so close on the edge of the orgasm that my body is starving for, and it's almost painful. His tongue begins swirling on the bud of my sex, and I groan incoherent words. My hands move to grip his head so he will stay right where my body is begging for release.

"You like me working your clit, Celine?" he asks me, while playing in the wetness of my core.

"Yes, yes, Levi!" I say in a rush of words, needing him to give me that little bit more to send my body reeling in rapture.

"Tell me," he commands.

I am lost on what he expects from me. My hands tighten their grip on his hair, pulling out strands until he moans from the unintentional pain I cause.

"I like it so, ugh…much." *Oh Deity, please say I said the right thing.*

"No! Say it," Levi growls.

My breath hitches in my throat from him continuingly curbing my orgasm.

Feeling completely dirty, but in a good way, I repeat his words. "Oh Deity, I like you working my clit, Levi," bursts forth from me.

He rewards me by continuing his maddening pace on my sex. "Mmm…good girl," Levi moans into me.

I cry out his name. "Ah, yes. So close. Yes!"

I try to move my hips, but he continues to hold me down. His tongue swirls faster and with more pressure. His finger teases the opening of my core. He slowly slips it in, and my slick channel clenches as he begins stroking in and out—adding another finger and curling them to rub against the wall of my sex.

I grind myself against his mouth. My hands fist his hair even harder than before. A distant thought pops into my head for a second of how he will probably have bald patches on his head if this keeps up. I cannot seem to make myself care about anything more than keeping him in the exact spot I need him to be.

Suddenly, I explode. My nerve endings are on fire. My legs straighten and my toes curl. In the span of what feels like an eternity and only a flash of time at the same moment, I am nothing. I am nothing but the continuous flow of sensation moving through me like the ocean's waves. Who knew this feeling was the reward for being denied immediate gratification.

"Good girl, Celine." His deep voice vibrates against me. "Come for me, again. Once is not enough. It will never be enough. I want to taste everything you have to give me."

His words heighten the intensity. Starbursts flash before my eyes as I fall off this orgasmic cliff into an abyss of unending euphoria once again.

When I gather my wits, I reach for him, wanting to give Levi the same euphoria he gave to me. He gently moves my hand away. The rejection, though small, stings a little—taking away from the intensity of my orgasm. Levi moves up to lie beside me and cradles me in his arms.

"This is for you, Celine. We have plenty of time to do more, but for tonight, I want to give you pleasure. To see you come apart under my mouth and hand does it for me. Close your eyes, baby. Maybe, tomorrow, you will forgive me my trespasses." He smiles while quoting *The Lord's Prayer*.

Time seems to stop, allowing me to soak in every detail. His chiseled cheek bones, with their light dusting of stubble, are rough against my palm. The heat of his hypnotic, molten gold eyes shines with male satisfaction. I want to carry this moment with me into the hereafter. When the forever fields of misty white and the unending lifespan ahead of me becomes unrelentingly monotonous, I will have this moment seared into my very soul to keep me living another day.

As I look at him, I want to tell him everything is okay and to please not worry for me, but it is not okay. Right now, I do not want to think too hard about all of this. I just want to be in his arms and awake in the morning with some kind of answers about my feelings and what I need to do. I lean in and kiss him. The taste of my sex flavoring his lips is decadent, and I realize my earlier worry was thoroughly blown to pieces.

I break off the kiss, and Levi pulls me closer. My head rests on the muscles of his inner arm while his other arm wraps warmly around me. He runs his fingers through the downy feathers of my wings, making my back arch in bliss. It feels so good I am practically purring. His strokes become steady, and I slowly fall into a dreamless sleep.

CHAPTER 13

"**U**gh...The sun is too bright," I say, groaning, as I slowly open one eye. My head feels like someone is stabbing hot metal shards into it. My body is sore, especially between my thighs. Last night's activities come crashing through my mind.

Heaven help me. I don't think I have ever felt this bad and good in my entire existence. Even my hair follicles ache. I get up and stumble to the doorway. I am still fully corporal, so I stand there, holding on to the doorjamb for dear life as my stomach swims with an acidic churning sensation. I walk down the hall, using the wall for support and follow the sound of voices.

"Daddy, is Ms. Celine getting up soon?"

Karina's exuberance makes my head pound hard enough for my teeth to ache.

"She will be up soon, Karina," Jake says softly and reassuringly. Although, I was pretty sure I was dying a slow death. Was the wine poisoned? Holy Deity, I hope I can make it.

"Good, can I ask her to take me to school like Andy's angel goes with him?"

Her pleading for my presence is sweet, and I smile through the discomfort hammering down on me.

"I don't think she will be up for the day-long trip to your school. I can drive you, and Celine can come with us. That's if it's okay with your dad."

The deep bass of Levi's voice makes my soul warm and my palms sweat in nervousness. *Will he treat me like a pariah after everything he confessed and what we did last night?*

"Yay! Daddy, is it okay? Please, oh please, say yes, Daddy."

I walk in and see Karina jumping up and down, her hair a mass of mahogany curls bouncing all over her petite frame. The apples of her cheeks blush a beautiful rose in her excitement.

"Yes, now go get your school stuff together."

Karina squeals in delight and runs for the doorway. The blue jumper she wears sways with her movements. I am standing in her way, but she looks up as she heads my way and graces me with her innocent smile.

Stopping dead in her tracks, she throws her small arms around me, and I barely catch my balance.

Karina sings, "Hi, Celine! You and Levi are going to take me to school today!"

"Hello, sweetling. You are so very enthusiastic in the morning," I say, fondly patting her silky fall of curly hair.

Karina skips past me, her voice carrying as she makes her way down the hall. "Yup, I have to get my stuff. I'll be right back."

"How bad are you hurting?" Jake asks, making me want to smack the smirk off his face.

I look at Levi and blush. Then, I really take him in, and it is not fair. He is bright eyed and freshly showered. His hair is still damp, and the light sandalwood fragrance of it has me breathing him in deeply at this distance. Him and Jake are both ready for the day, and I almost had to drag myself to get this far.

I feel like I was hit by a large vehicle, and I am pretty sure I look like a Gorgon with snakes for hair. Luckily, he isn't turning to stone yet, so it can't be that bad. I force myself to look away from him, not wanting to get lost in whatever pull it is that keeps my body and sight constantly gravitating towards him.

I answer Jake's question on a heavy sigh. "Is it normal for the roots of my hair to hurt after only drinking two glasses of wine?"

My question earns a chuckle from Jake and a heart stopping smile from Levi. Looking at his lips reminds me of where they were on my body last night. I lift my hand to my mouth as if to replay the way his mouth felt against me.

"Here, take this." Levi clears his throat and hands me two little, white pills and a glass of water. I place the tablets on my tongue as I have seen so many do before and immediately begin to gag at the bitter chalky taste. I quickly lift the glass of water to my lips and gulp as much of the refreshing liquid as I can to cleanse my mouth of the horrid taste. Jake and Levi try not to laugh at me. Their reaction is much the same as Marcus's when his lips start twitching.

Grrrr...

"Can I ask you a question?" Levi asks, still trying to hold back his laughter by biting his bottom lip.

"Um...sure?" This self-conscious behavior in me is becoming so tiresome. I can't keep being so demure. It is not who I want to be seen as any more. I am a strong female and a Watcher. I was chosen to regulate a demon half-breed because of my strength and fortitude.

Grow a darn backbone, Celine!

"Is there a way to hide your wings?"

Then he has to go and say that. Does the man have no regard for my feelings?

"Are you ashamed of my wings?" I practically snarl at him. I turn a look on Jake I am sure would flay him if it could.

His eyes widen like a deer caught in the headlights, and he stops sniggering immediately. He turns towards the dishes and busies himself by loading them into the dishwasher.

Levi raises his hands up in a placating gesture. "No, I just want to take you somewhere people are around, *en masse*. I figure the wings would be extremely eye catching. But, hey, if you want to flaunt them around, far be it from me to stop you."

In a small voice I reply, "Oh, well then. Yes, I can tuck my wings away." I twist the fabric of my gown in my fist. I can't go anywhere looking like this.

"Here," Levi says, handing me a bag with a popular clothing chain printed in bold letters on the front of it. The warm gesture makes me want to cry, and my lip trembles. I look up at him, and he looks a little uncomfortable.

"Karina and I will be waiting for you in the car." He quickly makes his departure.

I am left dumbfounded.

"He is so confusing," I whisper, mostly to myself.

Jake turns a dial on the dishwasher. "Aren't all humans?"

"Their reasoning can be truly baffling at times."

"Kind of like drinking wine when water would have been sufficient."

Sarcastic brat! "Please, refrain from saying that word around me. It makes my stomach churn."

"And what word was that again? Wine!"

Does he have to say it so loud? Jiminy! "Ugh…you are mean, Fallen." I walk away, hearing his quiet laughter behind my back and smile to myself. He really is mischievous, and I like it. Even if it is at my expense.

I make my way towards the little bathroom I passed by earlier while walking down the hall. Closing myself in, I relish the feel of the cool tile under my feet. I look over the sink and into the mirror, and my reflection is almost horrifying. My hair is an absolute mess of knots. My pale complexion is marred by the rosiness in my cheeks.

My eyes stand out in a jewel-like tone— emeralds surrounded by snow white colored lashes.

The pristine white, downy feathers of my wings peek over my shoulders, and I am already sad that I have to hide them. They are small and tuck away easily. Having to be something I am not to fit into this world and be close to Levi is putting a huge damper on last night's happy glow.

I quickly grab the brush sitting off to the side of the sink and run it through the snarls in my hair. It is smoothed out in no time, and I turn on the water and giggle joyously at the feel of the cool liquid running over my hand. I splash it against my face. The temperature contrast makes me gasp, but it is refreshing.

I see an unopened tooth brush and give it a try. Minty toothpaste is now my new best friend as I scrub the bristles along my gums and teeth, just the way I have seen it done for years and years of my life. I love it! When my teeth are brushed clean, and the mint makes my lips sting a little—slightly plumping them and adding a deeper coral tone.

I remove the clothing from the bag, pulling the tags off as I go. Dark denim jeans and a black ribbed tank top make up the outfit. Simple and no fuss. It is perfect. I find undergarments farther down in the bag and wrapped in tissue paper. I have never worn them before, and they do not look like they cover much anyways. As I slip on the black lace panties and matching bra, I feel a little naughty. To be wearing something Levi picked out and has had his hands on, something he pictured on the most intimate parts of my body, is arousing.

I stand, looking in the full-length mirror. My wings flutter as I take in my reflection. I have not put my wings away in centuries. It makes me feel like I am that much closer to falling, but if I want to be out in the world with Levi, I will need to just suck it up and do it.

I will my wings to fold in close to my body and retract into the hidden slits running along my spinal column. I try to shake off the feeling of restriction by quickly putting on the rest of the clothing. After a few attempts, and one hard crash to the floor from trying to put the jeans on two legs at the same time, I finally get it. I slip on the little ballet flats that are tucked in at the bottom of the bag, and I am ready to go.

I have to give him credit for knowing exactly what I needed and the sizes as well.

Is it because he does it for so many other women? Don't think of the, Celine. He thought of you when he bought these clothes. Just you. Irrational jealousy makes my stomach twist. I breathe through it and leave the bathroom after cleaning up after myself.

Walking my way over to the door, I find Jake standing there. His eyes express the same emotion I have as he looks over my shoulders. My poor wings hidden like a shameful secret. As if I already have dirty wings.

"Please, be careful. You're vulnerable with your wings tucked away."

His tone is paternal, and it irks me. As sweet as this Fallen has been to me, he is not my maker, and I can do what I want. Right now, what I want is just beyond the door. The thought of being with Levi makes adrenaline speed quickly through my veins.

"I have had my wings for a long while now, Jake. I am pretty sure I know how to use them."

"Yeah…make sure Levi doesn't drive like an idiot with my baby in the car." Jake smiles at me.

I wrap my arms around him in a quick hug. "I will head-butt him if he does," I speak softly into his shoulder.

"Deity, I would pay ungodly amounts of money to see that." Jake grins brightly as I look up at him.

I smack him lightly on the arm. "I bet you would!"

I place my hand on the door knob and take a deep breath. Today, I am going to just live. I am going to experience a day with the demon half-breed that has my heart and mind in a game of tug-o-war.

It is a new day, Celine, and you are going to make it worth it.

Opening the door, the sun beats down and stings my eyes, but even this pain is something I can work past. Pain is a reminder that, for this moment, I am truly alive and not just a misty form travelling between worlds.

Levi stands against his car, wearing his usual outfit of distressed jeans and a white t-shirt that pulls across his chest in the most distracting of ways. He drives an older black car, and it suits him completely. His masculine form against the heavy piece of machinery makes my body beg for his attention.

He looks me over from my feet to my head and lingers on a couple of places in-between. Our eyes meet, and I cannot decide if I want to run and jump his sexy body or if I should run as far and as fast as possible. He is a predator. By the look in his eyes, I know he will chase me and devour me when he has me in his grasp. Well, I hope that is what I am seeing.

He opens the passenger door for me. As I step in

front of him, he moves just a little closer, so I am forced to rub up against the hard planes of his body as I try to slide in. After I am seated, he reaches over and buckles me in. While he uses this as an excuse to tease me, I decide it is time to play this little game along with him.

"I am a big girl. I could have buckled my own self in," I say, using the sultriest tone I can muster and nipping at his earlobe. The vibration of his growl makes me put a little tic mark on my inner scoreboard.

Game on, Levi!

He stands up and turns away, doing a rearranging motion over his pants before getting in the driver's side of the car. This earns him a smirk from me as he folds himself into the vehicle.

Karina pipes in with her sweet little voice. "Levi, what kind of car is this? Why does Daddy call it a death trap?"

I laugh loudly at the affronted look on Levi's face.

"This, my sweet Karina, is a 1962 Chevy Impala. You can *tell* your dad he is just jealous because it's way cooler than what he drives around. Besides, I'm carrying precious cargo today, and nothing will ever harm you while you're with me."

I smile at him. He turns away quickly, a blush

tinting his cheeks. It is so darn endearing that I want to squeeze him.

"Levi, you are my favorite person, right after Daddy. Well you are kinda tied with Mrs. Davidson, but she bakes me cookies. Will you bake for me? If you did, you would probably be almost number one!"

Levi laughs outright at the little girl's ramblings, but I can see how happy he is and wonder what kind of father he will make.

"As you wish, m'lady," he says, looking back at her in the rearview mirror.

The tension after dropping Karina off at school is tangible. The entire drive to the bar, where Levi wanted to grab something from his office, takes less than ten minutes. In that time frame, we spend it passing furtive glances at one another. It is thrilling to see he is as distracted by me as I am by him.

The only distraction are thoughts of Levi's goodbye to Karina. Their interaction makes me yearn. I have no idea what for. I only know there is an aching. With her little hand swallowed up by his much larger one, he walked her to the chain-link fence surrounding the school. Karina threw her little arms around him, telling him he needs to visit more often in the morning because his death trap of a car is so much more fun than her Daddy's. He threw his head back and laughed, but promised he will try his hardest to do so.

He is so good with her, and his eyes watched protectively as she walked away from him, mahogany curls bouncing with every skip of her feet. She is joyful, and it was utterly breath-taking watching her look back, smile, and wave. She is a gift, and it brought the sting of tears to my eye. Tears I did not let fall. I thank the Diety for blessing the world with such beauty and love.

Levi and I pull up to his bar and park around the back. The trip here seemed not long enough and an eternity all at the same time. We quickly step out of the vehicle and stand for a moment, looking at each other over the roof of his car. An invisible force that magnifies every whisper of air between him and I steadily builds around us.

I turn, breaking the standoff we seem to be engaged in. It is as if we are both waiting for the other to make some kind of move. I settle against the closed passenger side door. The sun's warmth was glorious and I raise my face to luxuriate in the warmth of its rays. No wonder cats laze in front of windows, saturating themselves in the healing heat.

So many sensations to be thankful for, and I lose myself to those thoughts until I feel Levi's gaze upon me. I open my eyes just as his hand wraps around mine. The heat of his fingers entwining with mine, palm to palm, beats out the sensation of the sun.

A sudden pressure inside my chest makes my breath hitch. Never have I felt so full to bursting with a tangle of emotions. Not even those first moments where I was bombarded with the sensations from crossing onto the earthly plane. How does his touch means so much to me, especially after the much more intimate one we shared last night? Maybe Levi and I took a few missteps, but I wouldn't trade those moments—no matter the quickness in which they came about.

"Well, at least the Fallen locked up before running away with you," he says with an odd timber to his voice. Ruefulness, or maybe irritation, it is hard to decipher with him facing the door.

"He didn't run away with me," I say, matter-of-factly, but curiosity assails me. I want to ask him how he knew who I was with. I could have just traversed planes and gone home. "You know, I had wondered if I should ask how you knew I would be with Jake at his home."

"That is not a question."

His voice—light, breezy, and immediately suspicion—makes its home in my thoughts.

"I assure you, there is a question there."

"It sounded more like a statement to yourself," he replies.

You want to be difficult, Levi. Fine, be difficult! I think to myself.

"How did you, *Levi*, know I was with Jake and not in my heavenly home?"

He sighs deeply as if I am burdening him. Well, it will take more than a heavy sigh to make me drop the question. Especially now he made me beg an answer out of him. I look at his beautiful and utterly masculine face, lost in his golden eyes, while waiting for him to continue.

"I didn't know. I just hoped. I called, and when he tried to play like he had no idea what I was talking about, I knew for sure you ran away to him," he says, almost awkwardly.

To see him without his usual swagger is endearing. His words are hesitant at first, but when they come, it seems to be on a rush of breath as if every word has to come out at once or they won't come at all.

"I told him I was on my way to his house, and he dropped the pretense that he didn't know where you were."

A flurry of butterflies take flight in my stomach. Levi turns his face away, but not before I see a pinkening of his cheeks. My heart races and my breath catches in my throat. I am surprised my organs haven't combusted from all these unexpected gestures filling me to bursting with affection.

He unlocks the door, and we enter the dim, cavernous space. The only lighting comes through the slightly filmy windows, set higher than usual into the walls. I am distracted by the dancing dust motes twining about in the beams shining through. I smile, thinking this is a very close correlation to Levi and I. Myself dancing around Levi in not so invisible circles since he had been able to sense and see my presence this whole time.

The most inappropriate idea of making him a Maypole dedicated to fertility suddenly swarms my thoughts, and I blush. I'd been witness to the celebration many a time and remember the joy of those dancing with ribbon twining around them. Some were caught and bound amongst those colorful vines of satin. I shiver as I imagine being the one bound…

Levi glances at my face, and I cannot help averting my eyes from his penetrative, golden stare.

Oh Diety! My wayward thoughts have begun a

chain of pictures in my mind's eye to distract me. I work to forget scenes of being bound open to his lustful gaze, and there I go again. I groan internally and make myself focus on the here and now.

With his hand at the small of my back, he maneuvers me into his office and toward the desk. I run the pad of my finger against the smooth glass, over and over, in a slow, steady caress. The repetitive motion is calming to my anxiety. I've no idea the amount of time that passes while I am lost in the movement and feel of the cool glass beneath my fingers.

When I look up, I see Levi watching as I stroke his table. He must find me so odd, and that bit of self-consciousness creeps in a little to remind me of how different we are. He must see the need for reassurance in my face because he stands before me and reaches to wrap me in his embrace. The strength in his arms is grounding. There seems to be a sort of relief in his touch—as if it helps remove the tension that has been accumulating since this morning.

"I enjoy watching you. There is always this amazement on your face with everything you come in contact with. Must be a big change to be watched instead of being the watcher."

Levi takes in a breath and exhales it out heavily to blow the fine, silvery-white strands of hair from my face. There is a looseness to the set of his shoulders as well now. I think this embrace is helping him just as much as it is helping me. A knot I did not know was in the pit of my stomach begins to unravel.

I glory in this new emotion. His touch is like a steady burn deep inside my being, instead of the usual raging inferno sweeping through my body. Could these be the beginning tendrils of love as they start to entwine around us?

I am most likely reading too much into his actions. I may be ancient in years, but to go through this revolving door of emotions in this way, I may as well be in the stages of puberty. Awkward and unsure of my feelings and body.

I am astounded he cannot read the yearning in my body or hear it in my voice. Could he really think I would refuse his presence the night after sharing myself with him?

"Celine, I'm going to kiss you," he says with devastating simplicity.

I want to give in, but I think it is time to try out these new feminine wiles of mine.

"Are you?" I pull back just a little, my hands resting behind me as I lean against his desk.

His grip tightens around me, and the pressure is delicious.

"Yes."

"What if I do not want you to kiss me?" I say on a whisper.

"I would try to plead to your angelic nature. You wouldn't want me to be standing here, aching all day, would you?"

His tone is coaxing, and my body begins to bloom for him.

"As a matter of fact, I would."

"And they say I am the half-demon. You are a cruel creature."

"Very."

Hs lips are a hairsbreadth away. He growls and leans in to take my mouth, but my hand slips on the smooth glass of the desk I rest upon. A sharp pain lets me know I must be cut, and it was probably on the dagger he uses as a letter opener.

I watch with hooded eyes as he tries to control his reaction to the tiny bite of pain surging from me to him. It is erotic to watch the little bit of agony cross his features. He picks up the ancient silver stiletto with its bejeweled handle and looks at it almost hypnotically. Suddenly, he flicks the little drops of blood from it and releases me completely. Levi quickly steps back, a look of shame crossing his features. Before I can try to reassure him, a voice intrudes upon us.

Looking back, I see a man standing in the mirror. Reality crashes down on me as I realize this is no man. I am only feet away from a demon. A full-blooded demon. This is not Levi's father, not that seeing that demon would have been less terrifying. This is Zepar—the equivalent of a Duke in hell, commanding legions. He is sixteenth of the seventy-two spirits of Solomon. The trademark vermilion leather he wears, which is segmented for easy movement, looks poured on his lean physic.

Zepar is what the human populace considers an Incubus in their mythology. Here he stands, not a myth at all, but a demon of lust staring right at me.

"I felt your summons, Leviathan. What will you

have of me?" His words are spoken with such lascivi-ousness. "Please say it has all to do with this Angel before me."

A steady purr pours from the demon, something I feel more than hear. It makes me feel a little drugged. My nipples harden under my garments, and the material is thin enough they have to be visible. I do not enjoy this reaction at all. It feels like a violation.

"I did not summon you."

"Ah, but you did. With the blood of lust." His eyes are feline in nature— a kaleidoscope of greens, gold, and blues like starbursts beckoning me to fall into their cruel and antient depths.

He answers Levi, but the words are all for me. He wants to pull a reaction from me. He, of course, knows what I am. "Unless you called for me."

"You are very mistaken, Zepar."

After I speak the demon's name, I turn to look at Levi and see his body begin to swell. His veins strain and protrude as if he is preparing to attack. His face becomes a little more feral, eyes with pinpricks of crimson beginning to peek through. Surely, Levi knows Zepar cannot cross planes without a correct summoning. One he will most definitely not get from me.

"So, you know of me? That does please me. What is your name, sweet Angel, so I may know of you too."

"Don't answer him," Levi commands, stepping closer as if he wants to become a shield.

I am itching to tell him what he could do with that little order. I don't, only because I will not show a divided front before a demon of such high rank. I do not want Zepar knowing my name as it is, but it is not out of fear. It is out of spite.

Zepar analyzes our behavior as if looking for a weakness—like any general would do. He continues to push. "You would look magnificent draped over me, sweet angel," he says with a smile.

It is a decadent grin, filled with what can only be described as intent. My stomach churns thinking of what his wicked thoughts might be. There is no doubt I would be stripped, used, and discarded into a harem of those who have succumbed.

This demon is stunning in the same way that poison is. So beautifully tempting, I want to swirl my finger among the shimmery liquid or down it all in one shot—licking my lips and hoping I survive. Something so evil should have an appearance to match. Unfortunately, many throughout history have fallen to this demon and his erotic demands.

"Zepar, why are you here?" Levi, demands.

He has a look of agelessness, dark-skinned and smooth. I want to reach out to see if his flesh is as smooth as the glass I caressed earlier. I am not attracted to him as I am to Levi, but his looks are alluring. I cannot help admiring, although I need to run far and fast.

Once again, I rue that my wings are tucked away. Jake will no doubt have words about this if he finds out. Not to mention Gideon. I internally groan, thinking of the wrath he will rain down on those around me now. Thankfully, he is not looking our way, or he would be here now—especially with how overprotective he is of me.

"I did not use Malacoda's sigil. No being should have appeared."

"Is that what your sire told you? I am no prince, and only our higher royalty need an exact call sign. All I need is blood and lust upon the door. Just. A. Single. Drop." He draws out each word with heavy emphasis. His eyes bore into mine. "And to shed even a drop of an Angel's blood is a hard proposition to pass on."

"Leave, Zepar. On your own now, or I will send you away." Levi smirked, and a wicked glint crossed his eyes.

To be sent away is more of an ego check than a punishment. Demon or man, it does not matter, they will whip it out and measure. I truly understand the saying now.

Zepar's look is equally devilish as he leans against the portal, hands out stretched, making the visible muscle of his arms strain. A pose I am familiar with. One that gives the invitation to lean in and see what he may taste like. His desired affect is wasted on me. If anything, it makes Levi's rage rise a bit more. Maybe the real goal is to get under Leviathan's skin since Zepar dare not anger the Royalty he has to serve.

"Be careful, child, before I cross over. You would not want me to take that which is yours."

With my wings tucked away, I am as helpless as the average human, and my heart begins to speed up. Adrenaline begins to churn through my veins, preparing for fight or flight. My fists clench in leu of not having my gown to twist them into.

"Leave. Now."

"And you, Angel, do you want me to leave? I can make a trip to this side of the plane an educational one." He licks his full lips, pulling in the corner of the bottom. The look is flirty and almost demure.

I take a step closer to the glass. "How would you

conduct my education, Zepar? Can you trust me not to hurt you?" My voice is haughty, and I hope it irritates him as much as it does Levi. Since he says Angels apparently have an issue with thinking we are better than all else.

Instead, Zepar finds it amusing. *Will no one act as I predict? What is the point of being the age I am if I still get it wrong. I guess it keeps it interesting.*

"If you are with Leviathan, I already know a little pain with your pleasure is exactly what you need."

"Fuck this conversation," Levi blurts out and steps closer.

Zepar throws his head back in raucous laughter before saying the one thing to truly cause the most damage. "I will send your sire your regards and inform him of the company you keep. Until next time, Leviathan." Then, he fades out. Only the gilded frame and its abnormally clear mirror glass remain.

"Well, as interesting as that was, I am ready to go. If you want to leave and go back home now, I would not be surprised. Maybe, I can do some damage control with my father. No need to put you on his radar."

"Levi, I am not as delicate as you seem to think I am," I say to him, confusion lacing my tone. Does he forget who and what I am?

"But your wings are put away, and if he could have reached through and taken you, he would have. Now, how often do you have to deal with that?"

I have no response to his question, and he knows it. But he talks in hypotheticals. There was no way Zepar would have been able to cross.

Levi opens the door to his office. I walk through as he holds it open for me. The heat of his anger blazes as I move past him. I know the anger is not aimed at me, but it still stings like needle pricks against my skin.

"I will take your silence for my answer," he says, slamming the door behind him.

Maybe, he is right about me staying here. The thought of leaving him right now is a shock of pain. I promised myself I would not run away again. I won't, but maybe he needs space from me.

I follow him out of the bar, and he holds a package under his arm as he locks the door. I forgot the box was the whole reason for this side trip. The silence as we walk to his car is deafening until we hear the sound of a woman grunting. To the right, toward the street, a woman is trying to load a box into her car.

Levi practically races to the little lady. She wears the sweetest floral print dress and sensible shoes.

She has a kind face, and her smile is inviting. Even from this distance, I can see a beautiful glow beaming from her soul. By the time I arrive by their side, he has the box loaded into the trunk.

I look into her eyes, and with shock, I realize I see none of her life flash before me. I stare harder into their bright and crystalline depths. They shine like amber resin backlit. Deep wrinkles set into her face from years spent smiling do nothing to distract from the absolute clarity of her gaze. Like the seers of days long past.

"Do not leave him," she whispers. "It is not time yet." Then her eyes cloud, and they seem to match the rest of her now. She turns back toward Levi. "You are a good boy. Thank you so very much for your help. Go on, now. You have a much prettier companion to keep company."

I am so taken aback by this confrontation that I step away and walk toward Levi's vehicle. *What is going on here? Why so many supernatural like encounters?* I spent all this time watching Levi and never experienced so many events in such a short span of time. It has not even been a full day yet. I almost want to ask what's next, but I will not press my luck.

Levi must also think I am leaving because he

makes his way to me. His hand wraps around my arm gently with just enough pressure to get my attention.

"Are you going?" he asks in a tentative tone.

I give myself a moment to think through my answer.

Do I want to leave, really truly leave? If I do, I will not return—no matter the fires that were stoked between us, no matter the pain we will all feel if I go. I will even follow through with asking to be reassigned. The woman's crystalline eyes flash in my mind's eye.

"I was just walking toward the car to wait for you. If you would like me to leave, Levi, I will. I do not want to be a burden," I say with quiet and absolute conviction.

"No. Stay, please. I was angry earlier, but it wasn't at you. My anger was for me and you being put in that kind of danger. I'm sorry. Please, stay." He smiles shyly.

I am undone, but he still has more to say.

"I will even make us dinner. You do eat don't you. You drink, so I figured you might like to try some food too."

I take a deep breath and jump. This is going to hurt so bad. I know it, but I answer. "I'd love to."

"Good! I need to pick up a couple things, and then I can feed you."

The shyness recedes from his face, and I know that he well and truly wants to feed me in more ways than one.

CHAPTER 16

We are now at a farmer's market. One I have seen him come to many times before. The hustle and bustle of people selling their wares is a little overwhelming. I am jostled around by the passersby and little bits of their lives flash over me. So many lives in such a short amount of time make it hard to concentrate on the simple task of walking. Levi steps quickly to my side and covers my hand with his. The feel of his masculine fingers over mine is warm and comforting. He once again makes me feel safe and grounded with this kind and simple gesture.

People begin to move aside while Levi has me in his grasp. They make their way out of our personal space, enabling us to walk without being touched. It is a relief after all the lives I just sped through moments ago.

"What is your home like?" Levi asks.

It feels good that he wants to get to know me.

"I live on a cloud." I smile up at him.

Levi's golden eyes glaze over. His straight, pearly teeth sink into the corner of his plump lower lip. He shakes his head to dislodge whatever thought has its hold on him.

"A real cloud?" he asks.

I nod my head, a little distracted by a booth selling beautiful stones cut in magnificent pieces to be worn as jewelry.

"What do you do when you aren't spying on me?" He squeezes my hand, trying to reclaim my attention.

Hmm...how to answer this question.

"I visit the libraries or my fellow brethren, usually Marcus. He is...special to me." My answer is so boring and is a reminder that my life is an existence of stasis with no real change. Well, that was until the last couple of days.

"Oh..." Levi's tone is somber.

I look at him, trying to figure out why he seems upset. Before I can open my mouth to ask, he throws another question at me.

"Do you have a family, sugar? Like a mother and father, or do angels just pop into existence."

Did Malacoda not tell him about his life in the heavens? Maybe he tries to avoid the topic of his fall.

"We are brought into the light with a vast knowledge of our calling by our Great Deity, but he does not share his secret with us. One day, I awoke on my cloud and knew where I needed to be."

"The cloud you call home?"

"Yes."

"How did you find others?"

It is odd, explaining this to someone. I have never been around anyone who wasn't born into the knowledge.

"Upon arising, we are all drawn to the undying fields. That is where I met the two others who came into existence with me on the same day, Marcus and… Hmm…maybe just Marcus and me. It was very long ago. May I ask you something very personal?"

"Go for it," he says, ready for anything.

"Are you interested in having your own child? I ask because you are so sweet with Karina."

"Karina is an amazing little girl, so bright and full of life. She has a whole future of possibilities, and I would destroy anything or anyone who would dare try to take that away from her." His eyes are fierce, and his hand tightens slightly around mine with vehemence.

Levi will be her warrior, and it makes my heart melt at his paternal instincts.

"You have seen most of my life, so I'm sure you know I have never been with a woman for longer than a couple of real dates…. If you want to call them dates," Levi says the last part mostly to himself but continues. "I'm too afraid of passing on this legacy of eternal Hell and Damnation. To feed on someone's pain is a parasitic existence." He shakes his head.

The light dimming from his eyes saddens me.

"My turn to ask you a question," Levi says, trying to change the subject.

I let him, not wanting to see his crestfallen face.

"Why have you not been intimate with anyone before me? Like with that Marcus guy."

Could he be jealous of Marcus, and why does it make my heart flutter? I realize I have to answer him but the only response I have is a little too telling.

"I never experienced those…urges before." A blush heats from my cheeks down my neck.

"Celine, did you watch everything I did?" His lips

curl into a sinful smile. One that makes my sex tingle, knowing what that delectable mouth can do.

"You are more than a Watcher. You're a dirty little voyeur." Levi chuckles.

I go scarlet red. He makes me feel like a pervert. Maybe I am. For the life of me, I would try to look away, but I would always cave and be excited by the image of him finding his release. I try not to think of all the women he has been with and how inexperienced I am.

Do not dwell on it, Celine. You will drive yourself mad. Ask him why. Do not ask how many.

"The women you were intimate with, what made you decide to mix the pleasure with the pain?" I look away after asking and studiously observe a patron trying to haggle for a lower price on some kind of bottled oil.

Levi still has said nothing. I swing my gaze back to him, and his lion like eyes are already focused on me. What is it with the way he looks at me? So much fire crackles from within them, and it makes me yearn to burn with him.

"Will you be answering my question, or have I won this little get to know you game?" I ask as saucily as I am capable of, which was most likely just cute, but it earns me another soul-shattering smile.

"It kind of just happened one day. I mean, are you really sure you want to know?"

I nod. "Yes, I went on a small sabbatical to visit the undying fields for a month, heavenly time. When I came back, you were in mid-coitus and spanking a very…robust woman…with a paddle. Her name, I believe, is Isabella Marie Cortez."

He lets out a large gust of air, and his thumb rubs back and forth over my knuckles, the sweet gesture softening the blow of him telling me about another woman he once had sex with.

"She was the first person I fed from like that. The first time we were together, she wanted me to hit her. I just couldn't do it. She egged me on and on, but when she laid herself across my lap, she said it was just a spanking. One that she needed to feel good. I gave in, and it was drugging. Afterwards, my hunger was sated completely, and I could go for a month without needing any more pain. With the increase in hunger, came the increase in the pain level I delivered to the person I am with. I hate it." The self-loathing in his voice is overwhelming.

"My mother…" He pauses for a beat. The subject of his mother is a sensitive one, even ten year after her passing. "My mother encouraged me to not harm others. The need to feed was mind over matter. After her passing, I found out she would hurt herself while holding my hand as I slept to curb my appetite. By hurting herself in some way, daily, she fed me. Purposely stubbing her toe while we walked hand in hand, having me yank knots out of her hair while brushing it. I was young and didn't know any better."

He pulls me a little closer as more people begin to show up to this little outside market. The sun's heat brings out the subtle, mouthwatering sandalwood scent on Levi's skin. I lick my lips and hear his breath hitch before he continues to speak.

"I accidently cut myself in my late teens. It was deep, and the pain was…exquisite."

He shivers, and it is unnerving. I am still trying to get past that I fed him last night with my virginity. And, now, I am blushing again. I turn my inner musing off to listen more closely to Levi.

"Mother caught me one day and asked me why. Of course, she knew why but she wanted me to be open and honest with her. When I was done explaining, a look of pity darkened her eyes, and I didn't understand. When I told her how the look in her eyes made me feel, she decided it was time to tell me about my father. I asked her many times how she could go to bed with a demon. She would always make her face go blank and excuse herself." He sighs deeply and puts his hand through his hair. It falls back into his face like an obsidian waterfall.

My fingers ache to reach out and twirl the silky strands. His voice becomes smaller, and I strain to hear him over the escalating noise.

"She took me to have the scars covered soon after. That it is why I have the tattoo here." He lifts our conjoined hands to indicate the stunning and colorful dragon on his arm.

I look at the tattoo closely, seeing the raised and slightly discolored slashes across the dragon's hide and belly. Scars he inflicted on himself. Scars he is ashamed of.

We walk over to a booth selling little red potatoes and green beans. Though I am loath to let go of Levi's hand, I do, so I can walk across the way to a booth selling beautiful watercolor paintings of the female form. They are painted in vibrant colors to highlight the elegant curves and facial expressions in each individual subject.

"I would love to paint you, beauty," the proprietor says.

I smile shyly. Strands of his long blond hair blow in the slight breeze, making him look angelic. It makes me a little home sick.

"Very sweet of you to say, but no thank you." I

turn my gaze away, towards Levi, and watch as he hands money to the man in the booth.

"Are you sure? I can immortalize you. This face needs to be remembered forever." He grabs my hand, and I look into his bright sky-blue eyes and flash on his life. After a beat of time, I try hard to yank my hand away, but his grip is firm and unrelenting. My strength is once again hampered by my hidden wings.

The horrible man's name is Nathaniel Montgomery III, and these beautiful paintings are all of women he was abusive to. Flashes of every hit and kick he gave these innocent women are delivered to me in detail by the touch of his hand. The contact is making the visions so much stronger. I am nauseous as his touch seeps into my skin. Like the memories, it hurts and a strong urge to have him smited comes over me.

Nathaniel grew up in a rich, affluent home with a controlling father who ruled his house with a sharp tongue and an iron fist he used to bash his wife on too many occasions. It is now a learned trait in which his son engages in gleefully.

"Get your fucking hand off her." Levi snarls at Nathaniel.

His anger vibrates through me, so palpable it is a

force pushing up against my being and amplifying my need to strike the man. Nathaniel raises his hands to pacify Levi, the same ones that commit atrocious acts against such lost souls.

"I'm just asking if she would like for me to paint her."

He points towards me and a potent anger rises like waves crashing against a sea wall. I step closer to Nathaniel, not knowing I have until I am a good foot away. Levi moves in to stand between the man and I, acting as a shield. Fury drives me to reach past Levi to swipe at the rotten abuser and miss. This sorry excuse for a human need not ever put his hands on another woman again.

"She already told you no. That answer should've been enough."

We are starting to attract a crowd with our behavior People pull out their phones, and it dampens my ire.

"Whatever," Nathaniel says. "Take your bitch away from my booth."

I wholeheartedly agree… Well, except for the bitch part and only because I do not want Levi to get in trouble. But, before I can stop him, Levi pulls his arm back, and his fist flies into Nathaniel's face. His eye begins to swell immediately, and I cannot help relishing the pain that has just rocked the sadistic man. Levi shivers. I'm sure it is from the injuries he is inflicting on the human. I grab his arm and grip as firmly as I can. He looks at me, and for the first time, I see red veining seep into his golden eyes.

"Oh Deity, Levi! Please, let us go before you get into trouble! Please!" I pull on his arm even harder, worrying about this new development.

He takes a deep breath and nods. I take a relieved gulp of air and begin to step back.

"Yeah, listen to your bitch, you pussy-whipped mother fucker!"

The obnoxious tone of Nathaniel's voice was all Levi needed to hear. He is once again on Nathaniel, throwing his fist in his face and knocking him to the ground. This time, while Nathaniel is down, Levi delivers a swift kick to the man's stomach. The gleam of satisfaction is prominent in Levi's eyes. The angry red veining even more pronounced making my stomach churn at what he may be becoming.

"Levi!" I scream to get his attention.

We need to leave now before authorities are called. I cannot bear to see any more of this barbaric display if it means harm will befall Levi.

He grabs my hand, and we rush off the way we came in, swerving our way through the crowd. The sound of his motorcycle boots pounding on the pavement matches the thudding of my pulse. We make it to his car, and he hurriedly opens my door, practically shoving me in and slamming it shut behind me. I just barely avoid my leg being amputated. He slides in on his side. The car door crashes violently into its frame. The only noise in the vehicle is of our heavy breathing. His hands clutch the steering wheel, and it creeks under the pressure. I fear he will break the darn thing off.

"Levi, are you—"

My words cut off as he uses both hands to grab the hair at the nape of my neck, pulling me forward. Levi crushes his lips against mine, demanding entrance into my mouth with tongue and teeth. I part my lips for him on a moan, giving him the access he desires. Levi invades my mouth like a marauder, taking everything he can from this kiss.

He is so powerful to my senses. I grip onto his wrists, nails digging into anchor myself. All I can do is take what he is giving me, and I revel in his ownership over my mouth. I pull slightly away and bite down on his lip. The action elicits a moan from Levi as his inner demon feeds on the pain. I use this short beat of time to catch my breath. His eyes are their fiery, gilded selves, swirling hypnotically. The red veining is no longer present. My chest heaves, trying to catch the breath he has stolen with his kiss. My sex is slick with my arousal, and the need to be touched makes me throb.

Levi moves his lips down my neck, setting his teeth firmly into the flesh, and I yelp. He soothes the sting away with his tongue and repeats the action over and over again until he reaches my collar bone. My hands snake into his silky hair, and I pull.

"Fuck, Celine. I need you so bad," he says, groaning against my mouth.

Our shared breaths are warm and erotic as I lick at his lips. He lets my hair go, and I feel his hands travel down to the neck-line of my shirt. With both fists wrapped tightly in the material, he rips the top open, exposing my black lace clad breasts to his hungry gaze.

"Beautiful. You're so perfect, Celine." He shakes his head and lets me go. Quickly, he turns away. "We can't do this here. Buckle up now, Celine."

"But, but…" I stutter out in shock that he is stopping this from happening. "What is wrong with right here, right now?" I can hear the whining in my voice. I am changed after last night. I am this new erotic creature, and I want him moving inside of me, now.

"Jesus, woman!" Levi says.

I lean in and give his neck the same treatment he gave mine. *Mmm, he tastes so good.* I want to lick every part of him, I'm sure it could only get better after this little tease on my lips.

"No, I… No." He is growling all his words. It is so earthy, and my nipples harden painfully at the thought of his tongue teasing them like the first night we were together.

"You deserve better than a half-ass fuck in a parking lot, Celine. This is a place where anyone who dares to look into the window can see you." He turns back towards the steering wheel again and jams the key into the ignition. "No one is going to look at or covet what is mine."

Oh Deity! He just said I am his. The Neanderthal statement makes everything feminine in me pant for more. Once again, I am pathetic, but I do not care. I want him, and the passion he ignites in me. Who cares what happens tomorrow?

CHAPTER 18

Levi reverses the car. The tires squeal in protest, and there is a rancid smell of burnt rubber in our wake as he speeds out of the parking lot. I grip the seat when we take a corner too quickly. Adrenaline courses through my veins, making me shake with need. I decide to amp up this situation, I unbuckle myself and lean towards Levi. I run my hand up his thigh and feel the hard muscles under my fingertips jump in response.

I move my hand higher until I am rubbing Levi's cock. His rigid sex is kicking up at me with the mere stroke over the soft denim of his pants. Such a powerfully seductive high takes me over. Knowing he beat a man who dare touch me in aggression and is speeding to get me home so he can have his wicked way with me is intoxicating. My heart expands in hope that I really am special to him.

"You have to stop, Celine," he tells me while I caress his length, kissing and licking at the lobe of his ear.

I savor any taste of him I can get.

"Why, Levi? Do you not like my touch?" My voice is unrecognizable. Who is this sultry woman I am channeling? Right now, it seems I would trade anything, even my wings, for the chance to be with this man.

"You know why. And if you don't take your hand off my cock, we're probably going to crash into something." He presses harder down on the gas pedal, and we jerk forward with the sudden increase in speed. The engine revs harshly, and I can feel it like a beast under my seat. The vibration of the vehicle is enough to make me pant. My body is so much more receptive after our last two encounters. It is now priming itself for the thorough workout I hope I am about to receive.

"But you feel so good against my hand." I press more firmly and start to play with the zipper. I pull it down at an achingly slow pace.

"Oh God, Celine! We are so close to the house, baby." A light sheen of sweat begins to bead on his brow, and his grip on the steering wheel tightens with a crack.

"I can't wait to have the feel of your *cock* in my hand." I put a heavy emphasis on cock, knowing the dirty word coming from me will amp up his lust.

"Thank fuck!" he shouts out as the car comes to a hard stop, making me grip onto Levi so I don't go through the windshield. He opens the door and pulls me out the driver's side. Levi picks me up and throws me over his shoulder. He smacks my bottom, and we both moan at the delicious sting. Instead of him possibly kicking the door down, I try my hardest to focus so I can I mist us both into his place.

"Why the hell didn't you do that earlier?"

He snarls as I slip down the front of his body. My feet barely hit the floor before his hands are back on me.

"Because you were driving."

My words come out sounding garbled as he thrusts his tongue into my mouth. His lips are fierce on my own. This explosion of passion is everything I did not know I wanted. This is so much more than any daydream I can come up with. This is what all my watching of others did not prepare me for.

Levi's hands travel over my body, leaving electric tingles along the way. I slip my torn top off while he is ripping open my jeans. I want every bit of my flesh exposed for his persistent exploration. I want everything he has to give me, but I want to take as well.

Sliding the denim down my thighs, I step out of them along with my shoes. He rushes at me, picking me up. My legs wrap around his waist. My back slams up against the cold wall, but it does not hamper the heat coursing its way through me. Our teeth hit as his kiss becomes all consuming. Reaching down, I shove my hands into his pants.

Finally! Lucky for me, they are already undone and barely hanging on his hips. My hand makes contact with his long, thick, rigid length. "Oh, Levi, you're so big."

He smiles against my lips. "Flattery will get you everywhere with me." Levi slides the black lace bra up, exposing my breasts.

My nipples are already beaded and begging for his attention. He succumbs to their request by surrounding one and then the other with the warm heat of his mouth, swirling his tongue and scraping his teeth all around the mound of my breast, making me arch. I grab his hair in my fists and hold him to me, not wanting him to stop teasing me with his lips.

He removes his mouth but works one long lick up the center of my chest and neck to settle at my ear. "Tell me what you want me to do to you, Celine. I want you to tell me in excruciatingly clear detail. I need to know you really want this."

I can now reach down and wrap his hot sex in my hand. I move up and down his shaft. The feel of velvet melded over steel makes me ache to have him inside of me. The crown of his member is a branding against my palm and moisture beads there. I smooth my thumb around it and push my hand down his length. I've seen this done, but it feels instinctual, and I react accordingly.

"Is this answer enough?" I say, pumping my hand up and down, cupping the head of his member against my palm and rubbing around it in smooth circles. "I want you, Levi." I moan as he slides a hand into the barely-there panties.

He caresses my soaking core, and my teeth sink into his shoulder. Levi's fingers are magical, playing in the wetness he creates with each glide against me. Slipping back and forth, he brings the digits up to the hardened nub of my sex at an unrelentingly slow pace.

"Please, oh please," I pant.

"That's not going to be enough, Celine. Tell me what I want to hear."

The tension in me rises as he sucks hard at my

collar bone and then soothes it away with each whirl of his tongue.

Fine! He wants me to say it.

"I want you to fuck me, Levi. I want your cock sliding deep into my pussy."

One of his hands clamp hard under my thigh, and I know there will be fingertip bruises in the morning that I will look lovingly on.

"God, yes, Celine. You're so perfect," he says while stroking himself over my panties and along the seam of my slick sex, teasing my core and making me clench in anticipation.

I unwrap my legs from around his waist. A look of confusion crosses his face and then disappointment. He lets me slide down his body, and I drag my hand down his chest as I go. I keep making my way to my intended destination, the waist of his pants in my grip. I slide them over his legs as I settle on my knees, nails scraping lightly along his thighs. The jeans get caught on his boots, but I do not need the shoes off for what I intend.

—so thick and long. A vein runs the length, and I want to feel it pulsing against my tongue. A slight feeling of trepidation flutters through me, and I wonder how in the world he will fit inside of me. The head of it is plump and the creamy liquid of his pre-cum pools slowly at the tip. I tentatively lick around the crown and savor the unique flavor of his seed.

"Fuck, baby. That feels so good."

Levi's words embolden me. I feel powerful in this giving of pleasure. Now, I understand why it feels good for him to give me pleasure and receive none for himself. Levi's hands hold the sides of my head while I give his cock long seductive licks. Up and down his rigid shaft, my tongue works. I cup and fondle his sac the way I have seen many do before, and Levi's hands tighten on my head. His toes crack from curling so hard in his boots, and I smile. I pull back and look up into his burning liquid eyes. There is a tenderness in them that goes beyond the fire of lust. I remove myself from thinking too hard about his feelings for me. Concentrating on the moment, I redouble my efforts, moaning at the wickedly erotic taste of him.

"Celine...I can come from just watching that pretty little tongue teasing my cock."

His hand wraps in my long hair like a handle as I open my mouth and slide his cock in as far as I can, using my hands to make up for the length I cannot fit. I pull back and instinctively swirl my tongue around the head of his cock.

"Yes, baby, just like that." His hands still holding my hair, he directs the pace of my mouth taking him in.

I pump my hands along his shaft and entwine my fingers to grip him more firmly. I look up. When just the tip of him is in my mouth, my tongue circles it, collecting more of his flavor. Levi is an erotic vision with his head thrown back, and his chest moving up and down at an almost alarming rate.

"You have to stop, Celine," he says, growling and pulling my head back.

I fight for just a moment longer, sucking hard as he pulls out of the warm cavern of my mouth. My teeth scrape lightly on the head of his cock, making him pant harder.

"I wasn't done, Levi. Give me more." I reach for him again, my behavior wanton as I practically beg to have his shaft stroking in and out of my mouth again.

"No." He picks me up off my knees. "I want to spend myself deep inside your pussy. You're going to feel every inch of my cock throbbing as I come." He holds me close, his arm around my back. His hand wraps around the nape of my neck. Levi pulls me forward and presses his lips to mine in a kiss so heated that my knees go weak. His other hand snakes down and grabs my thigh, pulling it around his waist.

"I have wanted my hands on this heart-shaped ass for so long now. The first time you bent over, I could see this ass through your gown…" He pauses massaging the firm globes in his strong hands. Levi reaches farther down, slipping his fingers through the cleft of my sex and making my whole body shiver in anticipation.

"Sit down on the edge of the couch and lean back with your feet on the edge for me, Celine."

Levi's command comes out silky smooth, making my sex clench in anticipation. He reaches around me to unclasp my bra. As it slides down my arms, Levi hooks his fingers in the black lace panties and rips the sides to watch them flutter towards the floor.

"Yes, sir," I respond on a breathy sigh.

Levi sucks in a breath between his teeth. I turn and walk towards the couch, putting a seductive beat in the sway of my hips, trying to entice him further. My hair swishes on the small of my back, adding to the teasing sensation. Walking nude with Levi as my audience makes me feel empowered, and I relish his reaction to the show as I turn around and see him licking his plump lips and clenching his fists.

I do as he asks of me. I feel the smooth suede

fabric under my body as I slide my hot flesh onto the couch. Leaning back, I open my legs wide and put my feet up on the edge as Levi requested. I feel so exposed and vulnerable. My toes curl under to grip the sofa so I will not give into the sudden self-consciousness and slam my legs shut. I feel the cool air against the wet heat of my sex and moan.

Levi doesn't suffer from modesty as he stalks towards me. His body is a work of art. Every tan, muscled contour of him is a study in the perfect male physic. Gilded eyes fixate on me in an animal-istic manner. Possession and dominance exudes from him, so tangible it radiates from his body in waves. Levi unlaces his boots casually and kicks them off. He effortlessly steps out of his pants, gliding as he gravitates towards me with his innate grace. Levi watches me like prey he is stalking, and I am ready to be the one he devours.

"I don't deserve to be here with you like this." He gracefully falls to his knees "You deserve better than a half-breed demon, and still, you are here."

Levi kisses the inside of my thigh, and I bite my lip, trying to hold back the moan he elicits.

"I am going to sear myself into your soul so you will always belong to me." Without any warning, his mouth and tongue dance their way through the valley of my exposed sex. Licking, sucking, and nibbling in choice spots, he devours every inch of my throbbing pussy, and I writhe for him.

"Oh, Deity, please. Yes, Levi, right ugh…" A moan from deep inside slips out, and he rewards it by sucking my clit lightly. "Levi!" I scream his name to the heavens. This pleasure is so intense. The pressure is even fiercer than the night before as he uses his tongue to lash at the bud of my sex.

My hands cup my breasts and play with my nipples, pinching and tugging until a slight pain seeps in from the action, making Levi moan into me. "You are fucking…God!"

Levi collects the moisture from my slit and slowly begins to move first one then two fingers in and out of me. He scissors the digits wide to make for an easier glide into my pussy. The dirty words are coming so natural to me and makes what we are doing seems more sensual and earthy.

He leans up, and I see his member hard and straining as he strokes it in his fist. He lays his shaft against my pussy, and it's like a branding iron making me his. He rubs the head along the slit of my sex, making it slick with my juices. Back and forth, Levi teases me until he lines up with the opening of my core. He slowly begins to push inside of me. The fit is tight, and I worry he will not be able to fully penetrate me.

"So hot and tight, baby. I don't want to hurt you." Sweat beads down his neck.

I follow the droplets as they make the journey down the smooth, muscular plains of his chest. Levi is straining to not thrust himself fully inside of me.

I am no delicate flower. Levi will not break me, so I am going to help him along. My arms reach forward to grab on to his backside. I pull his hips forward as hard as I can while thrusting my hips upward. The sting is sharp, making my breath catch and my grip on Levi tighten. I feel a trickle of warmth on my fingers and know I have drawn blood. My nails will surely leave crescent mark wounds. I look up to make sure Levi is okay, since he has yet to move. His head is tilted back. The veins in his arms and neck are straining. He begins growling, making his whole body vibrate into my sex.

Levi looks back down at me, and his eyes are glowing. Quite literally, they are a swirling pool of gold and crimson. Instead of fearing the change, I am entranced by it. Lust ignites my blood to boiling. Levi leans forward to grip the back of the sofa. I move my hands up the back of his neck to pull his lips down to me in a chaste kiss, when it begins. Levi starts to slide out of me slowly, almost slipping completely free. I panic, thinking he means to leave me in this state, when he thrusts back in all the way to the hilt. He rocks into my sex at a maddening and steady pace, but I want more. Harder, faster, more pressure, I need him seated as far into me as he can possibly be.

His thrusts begin to quicken as he moves deeply inside of me. *Thank the Holy Diety!* The decadent sound of flesh slapping against flesh makes my nipples harden. My pussy soaks his cock in even more juices. My sex clenches tightly around Levi's hard shaft as my orgasm starts to build higher and higher. How will I survive this oncoming release? A sensation this potent can only be compared to a small death. The French have it right calling an orgasm, *Le Petite Morte*.

"You feel so good, Celine. ...Won't. Last. Much. Longer." He punctuates each word with a stroke of his cock. "And I need to take you...hard."

The strain in his rumbly voice makes me drive my pelvis up into him, rotating my hips in small degrees.

"Do it, Levi. Fuck me...hard," I cry out to him.

He flips our positions. Levi's strength is astounding as he maneuvers around with his cock still buried deep inside of me. He now sits on the sofa with my knees straddling him. I look down to where we are joined, and my breath hitches in my throat at seeing how slick I have made his straining erection. Leaning back and placing my hands on his thighs, I tilt my head back—the long strands of my hair add to the sensation as it sways across my back. Levi's thumb begins to make circles against my clit, making my arms shake.

"Hold on to me, baby."

I do as he tells me to. I wrap my arms around his neck and lick his lips. He starts to thrust upwards into my pussy a few steady strokes before he begins to piston into my sex. My sensitive nipples scrape across his chest, and my clit is worked with the friction of his pelvis hitting hard and deep against mine.

"Oh. Deity. I…Fuck!" I scream as a white-hot, blinding orgasm slams into my body, and my wings burst forth from my back slits. Pristine downy feathers shower over us. I arch my back, arms open wide. I am truly soaring, though I am not in the sky, as Levi works himself in and out of my soaking pussy.

Levi's thrusting is becoming erratic as he pistons savagely inside of me. "Celine!" He growls, arms wrapping tightly around my waist and keeping me close. His body quakes under me with the power of his release. I lean my forehead against his, the sweat of our brows mixing as well as the breath from our lungs. I am so complete in this moment. It is another emotion I was not prepared to feel with physical release. My mind, body, and inner light—my very being— are one with his during this pinnacle of release. I hope it is more than an afterglow to having my first shared orgasm. Coming down from this sexual high is painful on my heart. He holds me closer sliding his hands through the feathers of my wings. Levi calms me, makes me feel at peace.

CHAPTER 19

"Levi...I..." I try to find the right words, but they escape me. I want to ask him what this means to him. Am I just an itch he is scratching? Does he see any kind of future for us? I feel vulnerable and am upset with myself more than I can voice at the moment. He has never even said there were feelings of love. Just feelings of want. What do I truly want though? Another question I cannot fathom finding an answer for, but this experience is everything I could have asked for and everything I did not.

"Yes, baby?" he asks while tracing soft circles on the small of my back.

"I—" I begin.

Levi cuts me off, holding his fingers against my lips and trying to listen for something nearby.

"What the fuck? Who the fuck are you?" I jump up from Levi's lap, and his seed slips down my thigh.

Deity! It is Marcus!

He stands there with a look so furious it would smote Levi if it could. Marcus breathes heavily. His nostrils flare, and the veins in his body stand out in startling contrast. Worry for Levi's welfare overshadows my modesty. Thankfully, Levi stands in front of me, guarding my nudity.

"Cover yourself, Celine," Marcus says, summoning a robe and throwing it at me.

The ability to make an item appear in hand is not something I possess. I slip the gown over my body. The material sticks to my sweaty flesh.

"Why are you here, Marcus?" I ask, knowing good and well he is here for me. I want him to say it though. I want him to look me in the eye and tell me I will have my wings ripped away, my home taken, and my grace extinguished for this indiscretion.

"I don't care why the hell he is here. I want you out of my damn house." Levi's words are gravelly and hard to discern.

"You need not speak to me, half-breed. What I am doing here is none of your concern."

Marcus's superior attitude does not help the tension, and I am pretty sure a brawl between the two would be cataclysmic. I have to stop this. It is time.

"It is okay, Marcus. I am coming."

I look at Levi, and his face shows betrayal. I do not want him to blame himself for my fall. I need to break from him. Knowing what I must do is easier than seeing it through.

It is for his own good. I repeat that statement twice more as my breath hitches I begin say the words that will forever haunt me.

"Why would I stay here with this demon? Why would I sacrifice my home and brethren for one mere act of coitus?" My tone is nonchalant.

The look on Levi's face is devastating. His stance slumps ever so slightly in disappointment, something I learned from the years of watching him. He clenches his fists as his eyes meet mine, and he nods his head once as if in agreement.

He looks away with a slice of his head. A growl emanates from deep in his chest. Levi's usually gilded eyes are veined in red and are narrowing on Marcus. He brings a hand up to his lips and slips a finger inside, sucking and pulling the digit out with a pop.

"You tasted so good, Celine, fresh and sweet," Levi says.

"That is enough." Marcus's wings flare in anger. An emotion I have never once seen on his ethereal face.

His quicksilver eyes are void of everything but his absolute ferocity. He is terrifying and majestic, a being to bow before while begging forgiveness.

"Let us leave, Marcus. Now!" I stride briskly over to him with my head held high. There will be no walk of shame for me, even though I know exactly what I look like. A mess.

My gait is wobbly, and I have "just-fucked hair" as I have heard it referred to on numerous occasions. When I slip my hand in Marcus's, a look of confusion tightens the corners of his eyes. I lean up and peck him on the cheek.

"I have missed you. Please take me home."

"Yes, sweetling." He tilts his head.

I look back at Levi. His jaw ticks as he grinds his teeth together, and his eyes go full blown crimson, swirling with malice. Shutting my eyes, I breathe deeply, feeling the shift as we pass through the veil.

Oh Deity, the pain, is like being ripped in two. I leave the other half of me behind to save him, to save his future.

Looking around, I realize I am standing in Marcus's cloud. I try to yank away from his hold on me.

"I do not want to be here, Marcus. Let my hand go, so I may go home."

Anger is still prominent in the quicksilver depths of his eyes. "I cannot do that, Celine. I am to bring you before the Council."

"Then take me and be done with it." I almost scream at him. Too many emotions flow through my being. I turn it into anger because I have to leave my home. I am livid that I have to leave Levi and Marcus, my friend and mentor.

"I just want to spend a moment with you before you are gone from me forever. I love you, Celine. You and I were brought into this existence together, and now, you will no longer even live in my memories."

Marcus's words are fraught with pain I cannot deal with. It is just one more thing to push me over the edge of my own sanity.

"I am *so* sorry, Marcus," I say sharply, not meaning to. It comes out that way, and I cannot take it back, nor do I want to.

"Will you go to him when you fall?"

Marcus's voice is calm, bringing my ire to calm as

well. Guilt swirls through me. The troubled and saddened look that falls across his face makes my chest tighten. I give into his question and answer the way I feel—like my heart is shredded into tiny bits of confetti to scatter across the winds.

"No. I will not burden him with guilt. He is good. I have seen him work so hard over the last twenty human years to make it to heaven's undying lands. I will not jeopardize his soul." The tears I am trying to hold back are audible in the cracking of my voice, and I pinch myself to transform my pain into something much more manageable.

"Celine, there are things you do not know, and I will suffer the same fate if I tell you."

His words are ridiculous. We are both Watchers. Our callings are exactly the same. He only has seniority over me because he is gifted with other talents as well.

"What in the heavens can you know that I do not?" I ask. My tone is flat, remembering the conversation Jake and Levi had about me being naïve. About how I did not have a high enough rank to know what was going on behind the scenes.

"Kiss me, Celine," Marcus says quickly.

I panic as he pulls me to him.

"I…Marcus, I cannot."

More hurt enters his eyes, but he presses his suit and holds the sides of my face in his hands with no way for me to escape.

"Mar—" My protest is cut off by his lips crashing over mine.

In this moment, memory residue begins to seep into my consciousness. As angels, we can block one another from touch-knowing each other's actions. His lips upon mine open the pathways to a stored memory of Marcus with The Council. One I am now seeing and feeling through him. The intimate action is one shared amongst life mates only, and it feels so wrong to be sharing this space with Marcus.

The Council room is an area of endless white, like all angel headquarters. The Council members float in the center of the expanse, in a half-moon formation. Their inner light is so bright it obscures their true form, leaving all to guess what these celestial beings look like.

"Why are you assigning Celine to Leviathan?" Worry laces Marcus's and my voice. He is panicking at the thought of me being near a half demon and the son of Malacoda to boot. Though he is a young boy still, one day, he will be a man and do atrocious acts in the name of his father. Marcus's mind is made up that Levi is going to be a lost cause, and it disappoints me.

"Who are you to question The Council? Our word and command are absolute." Their voices ringing in synchronization es echo through space and time, vibrating against Marcus's being with displeasure.

"Please, forgive me my transgression. I only inquire over the welfare of my fellow Watcher." His insides churn with fear over me. Marcus is in love with me, truly in love with me and hopes to one day be my companion, even knowing we are not life mates and that I may find the other soul that will resonate with mine.

"Do you mean to take her as your bonded companion? Is this the reason you refuse to inform your charge of her new duty?" He swallows back the vile taste of bile that forces its way up his throat on the blatant lie. The burning discomfort seems magnified in the presence of The Council.

"No, Celine is not experienced in dealings with demons, be it half or full." A truth. Well, a half-truth, so the burn is not as bad as it was from the original outright lie.

"That is pleasing to know because Celine is not

meant for you. She is meant to tempt Leviathan to our heavenly ranks."

Marcus's confusion pounds as he tries to understand what they are saying. He cannot figure out if it is their words or the way they speak them. He can feel the layers of frequency trying to jam into his ear canal at once. I feel for him. Usually we spend only enough time in the Council's presence for a couple spoken sentences, only.

"I do not understand." He decides to come right out and say it, afraid of sounding like a simpleton but wanting desperately to know the my fate, his Sweetling.

"Leviathan is son of Malacoda, once one of our highest Angels. A Joy Bringer, he was stationed closely to Lucifer before The Descent. Malacoda is now a Prince in the deeper realms of Hell."

Marcus mentally rolls his eyes at the Council, and I snicker to myself.

Mistakenly, Marcus cuts The Council's words off again. "Yes, I know our history." Sharp pain lances his brain, and he falls to his knees, clutching the short strands of his platinum hair. "Please…stop."

"Then *please* refrain from interfering." Their superior voices are grating to both Marcus and I. "Celine was meant to be Malacoda's, Lifemate. With his fall, he forfeited her, but a part of his soul has been passed to Leviathan. Leviathan may have been spawned by a Demon, but that demon was once an Angel, making Leviathan half Angel."

"Half Angel," Marcus repeats in a whisper to himself.

I am in shock at the revelations spoken this day. Then pain, so much debilitating pain filters in through Marcus's memory. The fact has just sunk in that I will never be his. He will never be able to share his love with me. Instead, he will have to watch like we were made to do. It is our calling, and he will have to watch as I fall in love with another. I can feel his soul crying, and tears threaten to fall from both our eyes.

"Yes. You will see Celine's enthrallment to him very soon. She will not understand her need to be near him, but she will, and she will fall. You are to do nothing. Do not interfere. We need Leviathan to cross to this side. He will be of importance in the coming future."

Outrage replaces some of the hurt, helping us to breathe a little easier.

"Celine will be a pawn?" he asks as calmly as possible, though rage is beginning to build.

"No, Marcus. She will be with her life mate—the

soul that will resonate with hers through the eternities as decreed by our All Mighty. Will you deny her this?"

Shame that he would most certainly deny me this future momentarily flitters through, followed by disappointing acceptance.

"No, I worry for her safety," he says in a low and cumbersome voice. His hand lays over his heart, as if the action alone could hold it together.

"Do not worry, dear Marcus. They are both integral to the fate of Heaven."

Hope that I may still survive is strong inside of Marcus, reminding me of the angel I love like a brother. The kiss lightens in intensity, and I return to having only my thoughts and emotions.

"Oh, Marcus, you lied to them," I say softly against his lips as he cuts off the memory, not wishing me to see any farther into his feelings. Life would be such a breeze if I could accept Marcus as a companion. The thought is an unpleasant one, and I cannot force my heart to comply. Sibling love is all we will have, though at this moment in time, I wish I could give him more. I foolishly tasted pure passion, and it ignites my soul on fire, burning brightly in order to find its twin flame.

"Yes, I did, Celine." His voice is shaky from emotion.

"I am so sorry I do not feel the same for you." My heart aches telling him this, but it needs to be said.

"I know, and I know you never will. I have no idea how you and Leviathan will play a part in our future, but go forth and know your grace is lost for good reason. You will be whole, and from what I have seen, loved and cherished."

My poor Marcus. Tears gather in my eyes, begging to fall.

"Oh Deity, I…he doesn't love me. I have no idea what I feel. I only know that to be away from him is excruciating."

He raises a hand to place against my lips. I inhale his fresh, clean sky scent and blink, feeling moisture bead down the curve of my face.

"Please, my sweetling, remember me for I will no longer remember you."

His voice cracks, and I throw my arms around him, holding him tightly to me. I pull back and witness a single tear fall from his cheek. That one drop shreds what was left of the hold I had on these confusing emotions.

Am I to be happy that Levi is mine, as I am his? The hurt for what I am about to lose makes my heart lurch in my chest. My wings, my grace, my brethren, and my dear Marcus will all be gone. Two thousand heavenly years of existence just extinguished.

"Hold my hand, Celine."

I place my hand in his, and we mist together. The Council stands around. Their blinding, bright light obscures their true forms. For the first time, I try to look at them as closely as possible, memorizing the group of beings that will deliver my fate.

"Welcome, Celine." Their voices are harmonious in their synchronization and so lovely.

I sigh.

"We are giving you a chance to make a choice. One we do not usually give. You can stay here and keep your wings and grace, but you must stay away from Leviathan. You will not associate with him in any capacity. We will make it easy on you and remove him from your memory. Or, you can fall."

They really know how to win a girl over about falling, even if they do not know that I have been informed already.

I look to my left as Marcus grips my hand tighter. His eyes hold hope that I may choose to stay here with him. It is false hope. He realizes it, and the light slowly dims from his eyes.

"I choose to fall," I say with as much authority

and strength as I can muster, though inside I am in turmoil.

"Then so be it," they say at once, soft but kind.

Marcus pulls me too him. His arms wrap tightly around me, when as a collective, The Council beams their light towards me—lifting me up and away from Marcus's embrace. The tips of my wings start to burn as I float weightlessly in the air. The searing sensation runs the length of the appendages. I scream out in absolute pain. The sound waves vibrate everything around me. My grace is ripped from my body, and I feel the separation as my grace unwinds itself from its entwinement around my soul.

Tears flow in a steady stream as my grace floats in front of me, an orb of pure white light. I weakly reach my arm out to touch the warmth radiating from it when it floats towards The Council. I cannot imagine hurting more than this. How in the three worlds did Jake do this and still be sane? It must be because he has Karina, just like I have Levi. If he still wants me.

I look to my left and down to where I know Marcus is standing. His face is blank, though the tear tracks stain his cheeks. He looks upon me like a stranger, when just moments ago, I saw into him and his true feelings for me. I am no more. I am no longer his sweetling. I am no one.

I begin to cry again when the clouds open, and I fall through the veil. I flail, trying to reach with my arms and hands for home—a place I may no longer call my own. I've no idea what is in store for me. All I know is Levi is important to Heaven for whatever reason, and I will be the one to help make this future a reality. Should he choose me...

A SNEAK PEEK AT VIXEN

I f eye fucking were a sport, I would win the gold.

It was Wednesday, and I was at the gym, getting my sweat on. No, it was not from running on the tread-mill either. Okay, okay, maybe that's where about fifty percent of it came from.

January first had rolled back around and I, Lola Anabelle Marks, at the tender age of thirty, did the stereotypical 'New Year, New Me' fad. I made the resolution to get my ass to a gym—which I have been doing for the last five years,

Fast forward four months, and you'll see the new me. Five-foot-eight with long, dark auburn hair pulled back, soaked in sweat. My ivory skin splotchy and red from exertion, and my hazel eyes had that hungry look, because I was hungry.

I was down fifteen pounds and my curves had never looked better. Yes, I'm graced with curves and I love them. My larger-than-average breasts and bubble butt turn heads, and in a good way. It is all in how you showcase your assets. By wearing clothes that actually fit right, you can rock anything. But none of that described my current dilemma.

The other fifty percent of my sweaty suffering was from the massive crush I harbored on the woman in front of me. Yes, I was suffering. The only way I had found to alleviate the pressure was when I was at home, in the shower, in bed, on the sofa. Yeah. I'm sure you get the picture. If you didn't, I would have to charge admission for the show.

My god, I was sweating fucking buckets. I looked like something the dog dragged in from a salty rain storm. There my vixen was, working that bike like she had somewhere to be. I should have thanked her for the motivation to come. I mean, come to the gym. She was the whole reason I still came, really. I'm including my orgasm this time.

I watched her tight ass as she bent over the handles of the bike. She was pushing herself, harder and faster. Her movements made me so hot, I was practically panting.

Fuck!

My heart rate sped up. I was embarrassed to have visual and audile confirmation from the monitor on the treadmill as it beeped at me.

I groaned internally. A bead of sweat slipped down her neck, and it made my pussy ache as I followed it with my eyes. What I wouldn't have given to follow it with my tongue. I was a walking bundle of sexual nerves whenever I went to the gym.

She was about average height, maybe five-four or so, with ebony-colored hair hanging long and loosely braided back out of her face. Her skin was luscious mocha. Once again, I wanted to lick her, and maybe see if she tasted like my favorite salty caramel chocolate. The way the candy warmed as it melts in my mouth.

Mmm.... Fuck!

Now I was wet, so very slippery wet. I was sure that by the end of the little cardio session, I'd have flooded my panties. Oh, and there went another drop of sweat. It went down her back that time, giving me a new path for my eyes to peruse. I wanted to follow it with my tongue, lick and nip at her, as the bead of moisture slid down her spine.

Grrrr... I needed to get laid, *bad.*

There she went, climbing off the recumbent bike. I could tell you exactly what she would do next with my eyes closed, but I would much rather watch, and I did. She bent over and stretched.

That's right stretch those hamstrings. Grab those ankles. Yikes...

I shook my head at how I had just perved myself out. This was so sad. My vixen turned suddenly and looked in my direction.

Crap! I think she caught me.

The impish smile on her face made it pretty obvious that she had seen me eye fucking her.

Wow!

My vixen's bedroom eyes were a sexy, smoldering amber. Her soft, pouty lips were perfect for sinking my teeth into. I wanted her so bad that I vibrated in anxiousness. She turned her smoldering gaze in another direction, and I finally let loose the breath I hadn't known I was holding.

My vixen walked away to work on other machines, releasing me from the gravitational pull of her lovely eyes.

God! The humiliation...

I decided it was time for me to take off. I had already embarrassed myself enough with the staring.

I still had a client I needed to meet on the very outskirts of town. The couple had just moved here from New Orleans, Louisiana, and needed some help in the organizational department.

I headed to the locker room and grabbed my belongings. I knew the showers would be pretty vacant given the time of day, and I needed to wash the stink off. I lost myself in thought for a moment, thinking over what I needed for my clients.

I'm one of many Professional Organizers here in San Francisco. My job is to help people reclaim their lives from clutter, and I love it. Everything has a place, and I would damn well show them where that is. First, a shower was in order, since I was meeting with my new, 'potential' clients, I should say. I hadn't landed the job yet, but I knew it was mine. I'm awesome when it comes to working relationships.

Being that it was so late in the day, I had to shower at the gym. It wasn't a pleasant idea. I really needed to take the edge off from watching Little Miss Vixen on the damn bike.

She was made to peel lycra and spandex off of, and that day had been no exception. Tight, black, short shorts and neon green sports top had clung to her like a second skin.

Crap, I need to get out of here.

I didn't even know her name, and that was probably a good thing. I wouldn't have wanted anyone reporting back to her that I had been screaming it a bit too often at night.

Come on, Lola, get it together.

I started to disrobe by the locker, putting my sweaty, stinky clothes into their designated laundry bag, and grabbed my towels. This gym had locker room style showers, so they were stall-less. It was a good thing I loved my curves, and that the gym was pretty empty around that time. Situations like that have the markings of awkward written all over them.

I turned the single nozzle and blasted the water to get some heat going. Stepping under the warm spray, I started to soap my hair and body as quickly as possible before I gave into the temptation of some self-love in a public place.

Turning around, I tipped my head back to rinse. I opened my eyes and found that I was not alone. There, just across the way, stood my Vixen. She was completely nude—as in no clothes, as in holy fuck I'm going to cream just looking at her.

Oh god, stop staring Lola.

I couldn't stop sweeping my eyes over her delectable body. My jaw was unhinged, falling about chest level at the beauty before me. Bountiful breasts tipped with dark nipples reminded me of tiny chocolate truffles, the ones that would melt in my mouth as they sat on my tongue. Her body was curved and toned, but it was her sex that held my attention. She was shaved smooth, unhindered by any hair. I was ready to drop to my knees and worship her pretty pussy.

My vixen smirked at me. Her visual perusal of my body was just as through as mine. God, it was almost tangible. Everywhere her amber colored eyes touched, made me feel as if it were her fingers skimming over my flesh, instead of her gaze.

When her sultry eyes met mine, they were heated. If anyone has ever had someone with bedroom eyes give you that sexy ass stare, you know what it can do to you. That look had me one good twirl on my clit away from coming. Man she gave an even better eye fucking than I.

"Um…Hi," I stuttered out, trying to break the spell she had put on me with just her presence.

She walked my way and stood directly in front of me.

Oh shit! Don't attack her, don't kiss her, don't lick her, and don't find out if she tastes like melted salty caramel chocolate.

"Hi…" she said in a sweet southern accent.

Fuck!

It was the first time I had ever heard her speak.

I'm a goner for sure now. That voice.

"Hi…" I responded back, again. I mentally rolled my eyes at how my linguistic skills were on point.

Her drawl, in just that one word, seriously did me in. Now that I had an idea in my head of what she would sound like when she moaned, I had become incredibly lusty. I prayed she wouldn't notice how my nipples beaded. My skin goose bumped over, and I had to squeeze my thighs together, all over one simple word.

"I thought it was only fair that take a gander at what you have going on," she said with her sultry southern drawl. My vixen stood on her tip-toes and leaned in, her warm flesh pressing against mine.

"I want what I see. I want those gorgeous tits over-flowing in my hands. I want your smooth and creamy skin under my tongue. I bet you taste good everywhere. Mind if I take a sample, something small to tease my palate?"

Oh god yes! I groaned in my head, but I couldn't spit it out, so I just nodded. She leaned in, and I waited for the press of her lips against my own. A kiss was what I had been expecting, but instead of her lips touching mine, I only felt the heat of her breath against my mouth.

I almost jumped when I felt her finger against my slick sex. Back and forth, she glided it, collecting the moisture. A moan unintentionally fell from my lips as she slipped her finger inside my pussy, as deep as the digit could go. She didn't pump in and out of the sheath of my sex, she held still, and it was even more erotically torturous.

Pulling her finger out of me, she stepped away. My vixen took the arousal covered digit she had buried deep inside my pussy, and put it in her mouth.

Oh my!

She sucked and licked her way around that finger. She closed her eyes, as if to savor my taste. My knees went weak and my sex flooded even more when she opened them to reveal something primal and instinctive. I was ready to be devoured right then without a care to who may be watching.

Jesus, how much more of this can I take? I was so freaking close to begging.

"That tasted even better than I've imagined it would," she sighed and walked off to one of the other shower heads.

At this point, I really didn't know what to do, so I

finished rinsing, wrapped myself in a towel and looked back. Her eyes were closed, and her head was tipped back away from the water. The sight of her there made my heart skip a beat.

She is so damn fine.

I turned and walk-ran out. I still had somewhere I needed to be.

Where did I have to be? Oh yeah, with clients.

I stood in front of the sink looking into the mirror that hung above it. After drying off, I threw on an ensemble of a black pencil skirt and white button-down top tucked in. I rushed to french-braid my hair back, trying my damnedest not to think of my vixen. I threw on some mascara and some tinted lip balm and high-tailed it out of there. No need to go back into the showers and give her the best time of her life. No Ma'am! I had a job to do, but when I was at home alone, I would think back on every little detail.

CONTINUE READING VIXEN...

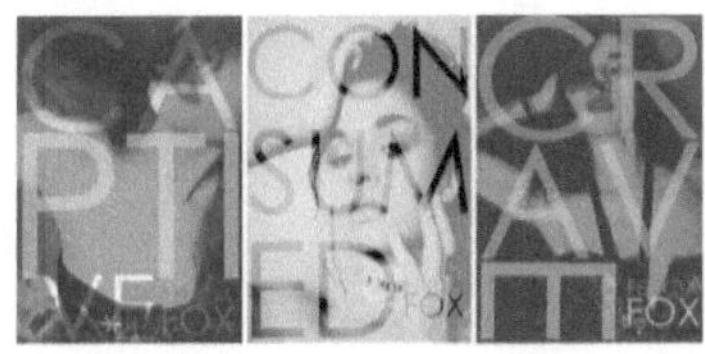

Come, take a journey with Felicity as she falls deeper down the rabbit hole, into the dark and erotic succubus world of Alex. Secrets, lies, and betrayal at every turn cannot stop their passion from consuming them. Will their love for each other conquer all, or will they meet their end at the hands of a madman?

Aine is stress incarnate, and at the moment she's at an all-time high. She's dreamt of owning her little donut shop forever, but as they say in business, "Location, location, location!" Right now, location is something Aine doesn't have. For the last month she's started to contemplate doing something out of character. She needs some relief from the daily "What the f**k did I think I was doing" rattling around in her head.

In walks Cian. There's something about this man who comes in like a flirtatious whirlwind that makes Aine want to be banged like a screen door in a hurricane. He's the exact kind of drama she doesn't need in her life. "All work and no fun" will be Aine's motto until she can pull herself out of the mess she's in. Is giving in to Cian what she needs? She's sure as hell hoping it is.

Carrie Lewis had a seven-year plan…

1.Graduate from Columbia University.

2.Intern at Lewis, Lewis, and Armstrong. (Her parent's Law firm)

3.Make Partner. (At said firm)

4.Work for a few years.

5.Buy a house.

6.Get married??? Maybe…

Ryan Pelt is a bit of mystery and Carrie can see not only does he have cinder block walls for an emotional barrier but he covered the whole area with barbed wire. Fortunately for her, Ryan is kind of a d**k so she had been able to talk down the hormones from an, "I am woman hear me roar.", to a kitten who purrs for little attention. Even though she knows all of this about him, a small secret part of her wishes he would throw her on a desk and make her scream out his name.

But even some of the best laid plans can hit a snag. Her snag just happened to be six feet tall with dark hair and the dreamiest bedroom eyes.

EMMA

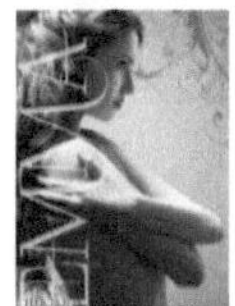

Lucy is tired of the ins and outs of the King family. Their prudish views on how one must behave in the public eye is keeping her true nature caged. At the suggestion of a mysterious, little black business card, she will soon find out what she truly desires. Will the acceptance of this invitation take her to erotic heights she has only dreamed of, or will she be left wanting?

She was that feeling. That stomach drop feeling when you're falling with arms spread wide in fierce elation.

That's what she was. She was that drop. She was a roller coaster who sent me over the edge time and time again.

It wasn't long before I gave to her, took from her. Pressing my lips to hers and capturing her moans in my mouth. She burned me, my beautiful surprise.

She will never know how much of me already belongs to her.

My love, my heart.

For her, always.

I spent years trying not to think of the way her body felt against mine. She was a delicious part of my past and one of my best friends. It didn't go unnoticed by my husband, how my eyes tended to linger on Jillian. His sexy smirk would make me blush furiously no matter how many times he caught me. Tonight, was our anniversary and I wanted to give him something he's fantasized about. Secretly I had been fantasizing too.

ABOUT THE AUTHOR

Felicia Fox hails from Northern California. She has her Associate's degree in Applied Sciences, but has always known she wanted to be an author. A lover of arts and crafts, pin up looks, and avid reader, Felicia enjoys spending time with her husband and two children. The Consumed Series, Vixen, Donut Go Breaking My Heart, Don't Be A D**k and Emma are her published titles. She also has an Anthology short, "He Said Yes," in Naughty Bedtime Stories (Second Chances) and Mermaid Water (30 Dirty Martinis)

ACKNOWLEDGMENTS

To my husband, for supporting me fully on this crazy literary journey, I love you.

To the amazing beta readers who took the time to "lovingly" critique for me. Thank you!

To Kristen Hope Mazzola, for always pulling my a** out of the fire. You are so damn wonderful!

To Catherine, for taking the time to teach me not just tell me.

To Sarah, thank you for taking a chance on me.